Mirror

by
Tanya M. Henderson

I would like to thank my husband Sam for his love and support. I would also like to thank him for helping me edit this book.

I would also like to thank Robyn Spengler for her final edit and publishing this book for me. Also I would like to thank her for help with the cover design.

Chapter 1

Inside the Mirror

It was a cold and stormy night. Megan was sitting on the ground in deep meditation. She opened her eyes and looked into the fire. At that moment she came to the conclusion that she was the only one who could stop the terror that was about to begin. She went into her cabin and took down the old magic book, which had been passed down through the generations of the Sapphire family. She opened the old leather cover of the book to find the spell to stop vampires.

"To kill the vampire you have to complete the ritual of the silver stiletto dagger.
Find the vampire before he feeds.
Beware of the vampire's curse.
The vampire of the ancient will charm you
 into falling in love with him,
 going to his bed
and accepting his seed.
If this should happen, you will become his and be powerless against him."

Megan went to the wooden shelf in the corner of the room and took down a polished glass box. Inside the box was a silver dagger. She opened the cover and took it out. She carefully examined it as she went back to the magic book. She read with fear what she had to do next. Megan took the dagger and sliced her hand with the blade so that the Sapphire blood would be the power that flowed through the dagger.

As the blood ran down her hand, Megan closed her eyes and called the vampire's name. She could see him. He was tall, well-built and charming. He looked at her with his piercing eyes. Megan knew that he was very dangerous and that he could not be trusted. She had seen this vampire kill before, long ago...

He was charming a young girl by the woods. Megan watched from behind a tree as the vampire swung the girl into the air. The girl laughed and the man laughed, then Megan's heart skipped a beat. The playing and laughing stopped and fright took its place. The man's eyes become black as the night sky and he bared his sharp fangs and bit into the girl's neck. Megan run to save the girl, but it was too late. She could see the little body jerk as the monster drank and drained her of life liquid. When he was done feeding, he ripped a piece of her flowered dress and wiped her blood from his mouth.

Megan opened her eyes and then closed them again. She meditated on her next vision.

Megan could see a woman with blonde hair looking out a window. Megan could not see the woman's face, just her back. She was looking intently out the window and didn't notice the man sneaking up behind her until it was too late.

Mirror

Megan was startled awake by the ringing of the phone.

She sat up in her bed and reached over and answered it.

"Hello?" Megan said in a sleepy voice.

"Hello Megan, this is Sergeant Ruth Toshibalua, the police department needs your help," answered the voice on the phone.

"What can I help you with, Sarge?"

"I need you and Robert to help us with a murder case. Can you meet Sarah at City Park?"

"Sure, we'll be there as soon as we can," Megan said and then hung up the phone and called Robert.

Chapter 2

Megan felt the warm air and the sun shining on her face when she got out of the car. She sniffed the air. She smelled the sweet fragrance of the flowers in the park. It seemed like a peaceful day, just like when she ran through the park on her days off. But it was seven in the morning and she was looking down at a woman's body in the grass.

The dead woman had blonde hair in a short bob. The woman was young. She was wearing a skin tight black dress cut low in the front that revealed her ample breasts. Her eyes were emerald green and she looked up at Megan with an unseeing look.

"Hi, Sarah," Megan said when the woman who was examining the body looked up at her.

"Hi, Megan, are you going to be on this case?" Sarah asked and then smiled.

"Yeah, Ruth called and asked if Robert and I would help out. So, what happened to her?"

"Well, from what I can see, there is a stab wound in the neck and several stab wounds in the chest. It looks like the stab wound into the main artery in the neck is what killed our Jane Doe. She has no identification, no purse, nothing to tell who she is," Sarah said as she stood up and brushed a strand of red hair from her eyes.

Megan looked closer at the dead woman and, by the way she was dressed, and came to the conclusion that she may have been a prostitute.

"It looks like she was a hooker and the john got scared and killed her," said a tall man with short brown wavy hair. He was dressed in a tight fitting black suit.

"Why do you say that?" Megan asked looking at the man standing beside her. She could sense that he was feeling cornered and didn't know what to say.

"Sarah, what do you think?" Megan asked.

"I am not sure if she is a prostitute. I do know that she is wearing diamond studs in her ears and a diamond necklace around her neck. Those are real diamonds. I am going to take our Jane Doe back to the morgue and find out more about her," Sarah said, while she zipped up the black body bag.

"Good seeing you Sarah, let us know what you find out," Megan said watching a fat man dressed in a suit walk towards them. 'Oh no, I can't deal with that son of a bitch this early in the morning.' Megan thought to herself, shaking her head.

"Do you think we can hurry up here? I have a Fair to start!" yelled the man that Megan knew as Mr. Dillon. He was a head of the City Fair committee.

"Mr. Dillon, we are just about finished up here," Megan called to him, shaking her head and thinking 'what an asshole'.

"So, who found the body?" Robert asked a police officer that had come over to see if Megan needed help calming Mr. Dillon down.

"That young man over there, standing by the bicycle," answered the officer, pointing to a young, thin man that looked like he was in his twenties wearing a cycling helmet. Robert walked over to the man to find out what he knew about the dead woman.

"Look Detective, I have a music festival to put on today in this park. If you would kindly hurry up and clean this mess up, and take this damn police tape off of the trees I would appreciate it!" yelled Mr. Dillon pointing his finger in Megan's face.

"Look, Mr. Dillon, this is a crime scene, now. You will have to postpone the Fair until we are finished with our investigation," Megan said calmly to the man that was yelling in her face.

"Detective, I need to set up the tables and the band stand."

"You will just have to wait until we are done here, or I am going to have this officer arrest you for interfering in this investigation," Megan said as the police officer escorted Mr. Dillon away to his squad car.

"The witness said that he was riding his bike and found the body this morning. He also said that he was the only one in the park when he discovered her," Robert said when he walked up to Megan.

"Well, we don't have much to go on, then. The police didn't find anything, either," Megan said and then let out a defeated sigh.

"Detectives, the Sergeant wants to see you at the station when you get done here," called the officer that escorted Mr. Dillon away from the crime scene.

"Tell her we're leaving now," Megan called back.

"It looks like we are done here, for now," Megan said to Robert as they walked to their cars to leave.

Chapter 3

"Welcome back, Detectives," said a red haired, plain looking woman dressed in a police uniform sitting behind the front desk. She was taking a photo of a man with tattoos all over his body.

"Thanks, Becky," said Megan as she and Robert made their way past the desk.

Megan knocked on the door that had a nameplate of "Sergeant R. Toshibalua".

"Come in," called a woman's voice.

Megan opened the door and she and Robert entered the room. A black woman was sitting at the desk, staring at a large computer monitor in front of her. When she noticed Megan and Robert she got up and shook their hands. Ruth Toshibalua was a tall thin woman in her late thirties. She was wearing a woman's business suit. Ruth kept her brown hair in a bun on the top of her head. There was a blonde woman sitting in a chair next to the desk and beside her a young man. Robert and Megan knew them as Candy and JP, when they worked together for the Denver Police Department.

"Hello Detectives, thank you for helping us on this one. Did you find anything at City Park?" Ruth asked as she sat back down in her chair.

"Not much, but we did talk to the young man who found the body," Robert said.

"Ah, what did he tell you?" Ruth asked, looking back at her computer.

"He just said that he found the body. He wasn't much help," Robert replied.

"Well, I may have a lead for you about our Jane Doe. Friday morning a missing persons report was called in, by a Crystal Stone from Denver. She said that her roommate Sharron Jenkins went missing and hasn't been to work, for two days before she called," Ruth said reading from the computer screen.

"Ruth, do you think that our Jane Doe and Sharron Jenkins are the same person?" Candy asked.

"It could be, Sharron Jenkins and Crystal Stone live by City Park. I think that we should look into it," Ruth said.

Megan's cell phone began to ring.

"I will be right back," Megan said before leaving the room to answer the phone.

"Hello...hi, Sarah...we will be leaving soon...yes, we will...ok bye," Megan said and then hung up the phone and went back into Ruth's office.

"Is everything ok?" Ruth asked when Megan came back into the room.

"Yes, that was Sarah. I asked her to call if she found anything during the autopsy," Megan said.

"Well what did she find?" Ruth asked.

"She called to say that she was just starting the examination and she would like us to stop by when we are done here."

Chapter 4

Megan and Robert entered the morgue to find Sarah examining the woman's body.

"We have a Caucasian female. She is twenty-two, with stab wounds in the neck and chest. I would say the wounds were made by a small knife or sharp object, like a pair of scissors. The fatal wound is a puncture to the carotid artery in the neck. The puncture caused an air embolism so that she could not breathe," Sarah said into the recorder in her hand. She looked up to find Robert and Megan at the door watching her.

"When did you guys get here? I was so engrossed in my work and trying to find out what killed our Jane Doe that I didn't hear you come in," Sarah said looking at them.

"What did you find out?" Megan asked as she and Robert made their way over to the examining table that held the naked woman's corpse. Robert looked down and shook his head as to say, 'What a waste of a woman.'

"Well, this is what I found; our Jane Doe's name is Sharron Jenkins. I took a photograph of the dead woman and I emailed the photo to forensics, they entered the photo into the Denver Police department computers. They found Sharron Jenkins' mug shot and police record for shoplifting; that is how I made a positive ID on who she was. It was a long shot, but it worked out. Now, this wound is what killed her, the fatal blow to the neck," Sarah said pointing to the stab wound in Sharron's neck.

"But it looks like a little puncture wound, and too small to kill someone," Megan said, shaking her head and leaning in closer to get a better look at the wound.

"Well yes, you might think so, but a small puncture wound to the carotid artery, can be fatal. In the dark ages when the Gladiators would fight they would take the point of their swords and..," Sarah said demonstrating the fatal blow with her scalpel.

"They would push the blade of the sword into the victim's neck and puncture the carotid artery. The victim would take a couple of breaths and then die," Sarah said as she pushed the blade of the scalpel into the wound.

"Also, by doing this, it cuts off the blood supply going to the brain," Sarah said looking up at Megan who was staring at the stab wounds in Sharron's chest.

"If that's what killed her, why stab her in the chest?" Megan asked looking back at Sarah.

"I suspect that our murderer noticed that Sharron was still alive and gasping for air, so he or she stabbed her again to make sure she was dead. When you are stabbed in the neck you are conscious for up to thirty seconds after the fatal blow, then you die," Sarah said.

"So anyone could do this?" Robert asked.

"Anyone that had the strength and caught her off guard could have," Sarah said. "They either knew what they were doing, or got really lucky. I'm guessing they didn't know the wound to the neck would kill her, that's why they stabbed her in the chest."

"I have to call Ruth and let her know what you found," Megan said.

Chapter 5

When Candy and JP got to the address in the missing person report, it was a light green Victorian house. Candy pulled her car up to the curb in front of the house and parked. They got out of the car and walked up the steps to the front door and rang the doorbell.

The door was opened by a blonde woman in her twenties. She looked like a model. She was 5 feet 6 inches. She was thin, without an ounce of body fat. She was wearing a black tee-shirt that was splattered with paint. In her right hand she was holding an artist's paint brush.

"Hi, what can I help you with?" The woman asked looking at them.

"Hi, my name is Officer Candice Carmon and this is my partner, Officer John Paul," Candy said showing the woman her badge.

"Are you Crystal Stone?" Candy asked the woman as she put her badge back into her pocket.

"Yes...Are you here about the missing person report I filed? Did you find Sharron?" Crystal asked with a hopeful look on her face.

"Miss Stone could we come in and speak with you for a moment?" JP asked.

"Oh, sure come in," Crystal said unlocking the screen door and letting them into the house.

"Miss Stone, I don't really know how to tell you this. Your roommate Sharron Jenkins' body was found in City Park this morning. She was stabbed to death," Candy said.

"Did Sharron have any family that you know so we can contact them?" Candy asked while she and JP followed Crystal into the living room.

"Please sit down and make yourself comfortable," Crystal said as she sat down in a wooden rocking chair, leaving the sofa for her guests.

"Thank you Miss Stone," JP replied in a polite tone, as he and Candy took a seat on the sofa.

"Please call me Crystal," Crystal said.

"Crystal could you please tell us more about Sharron?" Candy asked trying to get back to business.

"Well I didn't know Sharron all that well. We just shared the house and worked together. Our boss asked me if she could stay with me when she started working. At the time I was looking for a roommate, so I said yes," Crystal said.

"When did she move in?" Candy asked with a questionable look on her face.

"She moved in about three months ago," Crystal said and then smiled.

"Did Sharron have anyone that would want to cause her harm in any way?" Candy asked taking out a notepad from her purse.

"I don't think so. I hardly knew her. Maybe Mark can tell you more about her," Crystal said getting up from her chair and ready to leave the room.

"Who is Mark?" JP asked before she could leave the room.

"He is our boss at The Cowboy's Club," Crystal said and then left the room.

"Crystal, could we see Sharron's room?" Candy called to her.

"Yeah sure, her apartment is the first door to the right up the stairs. The key's on the hook in the hall," Crystal called back to them.

Candy took the key off the key hook, then she and JP made their way up the stairs that led to Sharron's apartment. When they opened the door, the entryway led into a carpeted hall that led into a small living room. Candy walked down the hall from the living room and came to a home office. Candy followed the hall until she came to Sharron's bedroom.

"JP will you check the office? I am going to look in here," Candy called to him from the bedroom door way.

"Okay," JP called back from the living room.

Candy walked back into the bedroom and went over to the bedside table to see if she could find anything to help with the investigation. She opened the wooden drawer and pawed inside. She found a notepad, a pen and some photos. The pictures were of Sharron and Crystal at a dance club, Sharron and a tall, well built, dark haired man, and one of flowers. Candy looked through the notepad and found nothing, just notes that looked like a shopping list. Then she picked up the photos and looked at the photo of the man with Sharron.

"I wonder if he could tell us more about Sharron Jenkins and why she was murdered," Candy said to herself.

"I really don't know if Mark can tell you all that much, but I wrote down his number and the address to the club for you. Also, I wrote down the name of the man that came here looking for Sharron last week," Candy could hear Crystal's voice coming from down the hall. Candy put the photos on the bed and went to the dresser. On top of the dresser she found a jewelry box, and a brush. She opened the jewelry box and found rings, bracelets, and necklaces. After looking through the box she closed the lid, and opened the top dresser drawer to see what she could find in there. All she found in the drawer was clothes. She looked through the other drawers but found nothing unusual in them either. Then she went to the closet and found dresses and clothes, shoes all stacked on shelves. After going through Sharron's room Candy made her way into the home office where she found JP in the hall talking with Crystal.

"Thank you for all your help," JP said to Crystal with a smile.

"Well, if you don't need me, I am going to go back to my painting," Crystal said about ready to leave.

"No that will be all," JP said and then smiled at her.

"Wait, Crystal! I do have a question," Candy said getting up from the chair in front of the desk and going into the hall.

"Could you come with me for a moment?" Candy asked before she could leave. Crystal came back to the office and then followed Candy down the hall to Sharron's bedroom.

"Who is this man with Sharron?" Candy asked and then picked up the photos on the bed, and showed Crystal the photo of Sharron and the dark haired man.

"That's the man that stopped by looking for Sharron. He said his name was Seth Brooks," Crystal said after looking at the photo.

"He didn't say what he wanted to see her about?"

"No, he just said that he was staying at the Sheraton in town and that she could call him there. He also told me that he was her boyfriend, and that he needed to talk with her as soon as possible," Crystal said.

"He didn't by any chance tell you what room he was staying in? Or how long he long he would be staying there?" Candy asked.

"No, he didn't," Crystal answered back.

"Thank you, Crystal. I am going to take these photos with me," Candy said putting the photos into her purse.

"You can take anything that you want. It isn't like Sharron is coming back anyway," Crystal said looking around the room before leaving.

'What a strange thing to say,' Candy thought to herself.

Chapter 6

When Candy and JP got back into the car, JP read his notes to Candy.

"Didn't it seem strange that Crystal could have cared less that her roommate was brutally murdered in the park?" Candy asked JP.

"Yeah, I thought the same thing. She is one cold fish. We should keep an eye on her. I think she is a sociopath," said JP.

"I guess we should go and talk with this Mark Willis at The Cowboy's Club," JP said.

"What's the Cowboy's Club?" Candy asked starting the car and pulling onto the street.

"The Cowboy's Club is the most exclusive gentlemen's club in all of Colorado."

"So it's a strip club?"

"Well, yes and no, the dancers are also models and actresses. I saw Crystal at a motorcycle show in Denver. She was doing a photo shoot and commercial there," JP said blushing.

"What you are telling me is that you're a fan of hers?"

"You could say that. But I didn't know she was sociopath back then."

"So, what did you find in Sharron's home office?"

"I didn't find much. She was very organized and very neat. She didn't even keep letters or emails."

"I found some photos in the bedroom in the night stand. But, not much to go on, except for a photo of Sharron and a man."

"Where is it?"

"It is in my purse, take a look. It's in the side pocket."

JP picked up Candy's black leather purse and reached into the side pocket and took out the photos.

"What did Crystal tell you about the man?" JP asked looking at the man in the photo.

"She just told me his name is Seth Brooks. He stopped by looking for Sharron and he is staying at the Sheraton downtown. I think we should go there after we go to the Cowboy's Club. Maybe he can tell us more about Sharron and who would want to kill her," Candy said as she drove into the parking lot of the Cowboy's Club.

Candy parked by a large neon sign that was shaped like a cowboy hat." The Cowboy's Club" was spelled out in pink on the hat. The only other vehicle in the lot was a black Lexus parked next to the door. Candy and JP got out of their car and walked up to the door to see if it was unlocked, but found it was locked. JP knocked on the metal door and he and Candy waited to see if anyone answered. They didn't have to wait long, when a short man opened the door. The man looked like he stepped out of one of those Italian mob movies. He had dark hair with a bald spot on the top of his head. He was dressed in a sweaty white dress shirt and dress pants that showed that he had eaten too many Italian dinners.

"We're closed! Come back at seven tonight, that's when we start letting in the public," the man said as he was about to close the door.

Candy showed the man her badge over JP's shoulder as JP placed his foot into the opening of the door.

"I think we will come in now if you don't mind," JP said pushing the door open.

"What the hell is this all about? I run a legal business here!" The man yelled as JP closed the behind him and Candy after entering the club.

"Are you Mark Willis?" Candy asked returning her badge back to her purse.

"Yes I am. What the hell is this all about?" Mark asked going back to the door and locking it so no one would come in.

"Do you employ a Sharron Jenkins and a Crystal Stone here?" Candy asked in an authoritative tone.

"Yeah, they work for me. Sharron is a bar maid and Crystal is a dancer. Sharron is becoming a dancer this week. Wait a minute. What they do out of the club has nothing to do with me or the club," Mark replied, defending himself and the club.

"These are the women?" Candy asked taking out the photo of Sharron and Crystal showing it to Mark.

"Yes that is them, that photo was taken for a promotional ad for Sharron to start dancing next weekend," Mark said looking at the photograph then handing it back to Candy.

"When was the last time you seen either of these women?" Candy asked returning the photo to her purse.

"Last weekend, Crystal left when her shift was over, about two in the morning. I asked Sharron to stay late to help Vic, our bartender, clean up.

Then I went back downstairs to my office to do some paper work. It was about six in the morning when I came back up to leave and found the club empty. So I locked up and went home," Mark replied.

"You wouldn't happen to have Vic's address, so we could go and speak with him?" JP asked.

"Yes I do, wait here and I will go and get it for you," Mark said and then left the room.

Candy and JP waited for Mark to return. When he returned to them he had a pad of paper in his hand and a folder under his arm.

"This is his work file, application and his home address, that is all the information that I have on him," Mark said handing the folder to JP.

"You wouldn't happen to have Sharron's information would you?" Candy asked hoping that there might be more information about her and her family.

"Yeah. Why? What is all this about?" Mark asked.

"Well you do have a right to know what happened to her. Sharron went missing after she left here on Sunday morning. Crystal Stone called in a missing report on her..," Candy paused to see if there was any reaction from Mark before going on. Mark just listened with a puzzled look.

"Well this morning Sharron's body was found in City Park. She was stabbed to death," Candy said.

"That's terrible. What a shame. She was a gorgeous girl," said Mark. "She would have made good money as a dancer."

"Mr. Willis, we wanted to know if she had any family that we can contact," JP said looking at how shocked Mark seemed.

"I will go get her file for you. Wait, I do know that she had a boyfriend, his name is Seth Brooks. Sharron recommended him to me. He is remodeling the club for me," Mark said going back to the office to retrieve Sharron's work file.

"I sure hope that file has a name of someone we can contact," Candy said to JP who was reading Victor's file.

"His name is Victor Marshall. He lives at 305CS on Colfax Street in Denver," JP read so Candy could hear him.

"We'll stop and talk to Mr. Marshall after we are done here," Candy replied while JP read the rest of the file to himself. He took out a notepad out of his jacket pocket and wrote the information down.

"I can't find her file. Maybe Sophia took it home with her to change some information in it. I will give her a call when she gets back from vacation. She should be back in a few days," Mark said, returning to the bar area where Candy and JP were waiting.

"Ok Mr. Willis, here is my card. When Sophia gets back, could you have her call us? Can you remember if Sharron mentioned anyone that had threatened her or that she was afraid of?" JP asked, handing Mark his business card.

"Yes, I will have her call you. No, the only person I know about was that Seth guy. She mentioned him to me when I was looking for an architect to help with remodeling the club. Sharron said that she knew of one and that she would talk to him for me. I was out of town when he came by to get the plans. Sophia met with him. She does all of the interviewing for the staff and dancers for the club and stuff like that," Mark said taking the business card from JP.

"Thank you, and we will be waiting to hear from Sophia," JP said as he and Candy made their way back to the door to leave. Mark followed behind them so that he could unlock the door for them. When they reached the door JP shook Mark's hand, after Candy and JP left. Mark shut the door and locked it.

After Candy and JP left, Mark called Crystal to find out what happened.

Crystal was in the art room, a screened in porch attached to the side of the house in the back, when the phone rang. Crystal answered and it was Mark Willis on the other end of the phone.

"Hi Mark," Crystal said into the phone.

"Do you know what happened to Sharron?" Mark asked through the phone.

"No. Do you?"

"No, we will have to find out."

"Is the architect going to be there tonight?"

"He is supposed to stop by and meet with me."

"Did you call about that little job I need you to do for me in Black Hawk?"

"No. I haven't."

"Did you tell the cops anything about Sharron or the club?"

"No, I didn't. All I told them was that you were our boss."

"I need you to dance in Sharron's place for awhile, does that make you happy that you are still our star dancer?"

"Yes...I will dance in her place."

"I want you to wear the Cinderella costume again. You will find it in Sharron's dressing room, which is now yours, until I can find another star."

"Okay. I am going to lie down until my shift."

"I want you to meet me in the down stairs office when you get here. Come early."

"Okay, see you then, bye," Crystal said into the phone then hung up. Crystal went back to her painting of the vase of flowers then made her way into the house to take a nap.

Chapter 7

Candy and JP reached Victor Marshall's address, it was a small house with a yard and a black Honda parked in the driveway. When they reached Victor's door JP knocked loudly.

"Who's there?" called a man's voice from inside the house.

"Victor Marshall, I am Officer John Paul and I would like to ask you some questions about Sharron Jenkins," JP called through the closed door. Candy and JP heard the door unlock then a man opened the door.

"Yeah, what about Sharron?" the man asked when the door was open.

"Are you Victor Marshall?" Candy asked.

"Yeah," Victor said then he smiled at her with a wink.

"May we come in?" Candy asked. Victor was dressed only in his boxer shorts. Candy noticed that he was in his twenties. He had messy blonde hair that looked like he just got out of bed. She thought his well groomed goatee and mustache were cute. He also looked like he worked out.

"When was the last time you saw or heard from Sharron Jenkins?" Candy asked trying to keep her eyes on Victor's face and not on his body.

"Friday morning. Why?" Victor asked and then yawned and stretched.

"Because she was found this morning in City Park, stabbed to death," JP said.

"What do ya mean? Sharron's dead?" Victor asked in disbelief and shock.

"Yes, and you were the last one to see her alive. What happened when you left the club?" Candy asked trying to read between the lines of Victor's emotions and reactions.

"I left the club and then took a friend to the airport, and then came home. I asked Sharron if she wanted me to drive her home, but she said that she was going to walk," Victor replied reaching for the pack of cigarettes on the counter by the door.

"Who was that friend? Can they verify your story?" Candy asked as she watched Victor light the cigarette. He was holding it up to his mouth and then taking drag after drag.

"Sophia, she works in the office at the Cowboy's Club, but she won't be back for a few days," Victor said taking another drag off his cigarette.

"Well, when she gets back we will have her verify your story. Until then don't leave the state of Colorado," JP warned.

Chapter 8

When Megan and Robert got back to the police station, Candy and JP were sitting in Ruth's office going over the evidence that they found.

"Well, we found out that our Jane Doe was Sharron Jenkins, our missing person, and how she was killed," Megan said when she and Robert entered the office.

"We found out that Sharron Jenkins and Crystal Stone are dancers at the Cowboy's Club," Candy said.

"So what is the Cowboy's Club?" Ruth asked with interest.

"The Cowboy's Club is a gentlemen's club, very exclusive," JP answered showing Ruth his notes.

"Who is Seth Brooks?" Ruth asked going through the notebook that JP gave to her.

"Seth Brooks is Sharron Jenkins boyfriend. He went by Crystal Stone's house looking for Sharron. Also, we found out that Mark Willis, the owner of the Cowboy's Club, hired him to remodel the club. Seth Brooks is staying at the Sheraton Hotel in Denver, here is the address," Candy answered.

"Okay, so, did you find out anything else?" Ruth asked handing the notepad back to JP.

"We did find out that the last person to see Sharron Jenkins alive was Victor Marshall. He is the bartender at the Cowboy's Club," JP replied putting the notepad back into his pocket.

"Well, go pick up this Victor Marshall and let's question him about the disappearance and murder of Sharron Jenkins," Ruth said.

"We already questioned him and he has an alibi," Candy said.

"Did you check out his alibi?" Ruth asked.

"We are waiting on that call as we speak," JP answered as he handed Ruth the information from his notepad. Megan and Robert waited until Ruth had a chance to read the information before giving their report.

"What did you two find out at the morgue?" Ruth asked looking at Megan and Robert.

"Sarah said that Sharron was killed by a blow to the neck, severing her carotid artery, by a small sharp knife of some kind," Megan said showing Ruth the report that Sarah gave to them.

"Why don't you two go talk to Seth Brooks, Sharron's boyfriend? See what you can find out from him. Here is the address where he is staying," Ruth said handing Megan the address of the hotel.

"Okay, Sarge we will stop on the way home, call us if you need anything else. We will talk tomorrow," Robert said as he and Megan left Ruth's office.

Chapter 9

Megan and Robert entered the hotel lobby and got in line at the long oak counter. When they got up to the desk, the woman standing behind the counter looked at them and smiled. The woman had long black hair tied in a bun and was wearing thick rimmed glasses. Megan noticed that the woman was wearing too much make-up. Robert thought the woman looked like a naughty librarian in some porno movie.

"Hello, how can I help you?" the woman asked.

"Hello, I was wondering if you could tell me if you have a Mr. Seth Brooks staying at your hotel?" Megan asked.

"Let me check that for you, one moment please," the woman said looking down at her computer and typing the name in.

"Yes we do. Would you like me to see if he is in his room?"

"What room is he in?" Megan asked and then smiled at the woman.

"Oh, I am sorry. We can't give that information out, but I can call him and see if he is in his room," the woman said and then smiled back after she explained the hotel policy to Megan.

"Well Faith, could we please speak to your manager?" Megan asked after she read the name on the woman's hotel ID badge on her blouse.

"Yes, but I am sure he will say the same thing. If you wait here I'll go and get him," Faith replied and then left the counter to get the manager.

When she returned, she was followed by a white haired man dressed in a suit. He was heavy set and sweaty. He looked like he ate too much junk food and he was eating a candy bar when he came to the desk.

"I am Darren Thomson. I am the manager. Faith has already explained our hotel policy, we do not give out any information about our guests," Darren said still eating his king size candy bar.

"I guess I didn't make myself all that clear, I am detective Megan Sapphire and I would like to know what room Seth Brooks is staying in," Megan said showing the manager her identification.

"I am sorry detective, I will get that information for you now," Darren said dropping his candy bar as he looked on the computer to find the information.

"Mr. Brooks is on the 11th floor in room 120. Would you like me to ring his room for you? What has Mr. Brooks done?" Darren asked with a look of concern for the other guests.

"Nothing, we just need to ask Mr. Brooks some questions," Robert said, smiling and giving the manager some reassurance. Robert took out his notebook and wrote the information that the manager gave them.

"Yes, if you could ring his room that would be great. Tell him that Sharron Jenkins is here to see him," Megan said then she looked at Robert with a sly grin on her face.

"Yes Miss Sapphire, I will do that," Darren said picking up the phone and dialing the room number.

"I am sorry there is no answer. I will call the maid service to check and see if he is there or not," Darren said as he hung up and then dialed another number.

"Cherrie is Mr. Brooks in his room...Could you check for me...floor 11 room 120...Yes call me back...Thank you," after Darren hung up he looked at Megan and Robert.

"The maid is going to check his room and then call back," Darren told them. It didn't take long for the maid to call back the front desk and report that Seth Brooks was not in his room.

"He must have gone out for dinner," Megan said looking at the clock hanging on the wall behind the counter.

"So what do we do now? Do you want to wait for him or should we come back tomorrow?" Robert asked Megan, who was looking at her cell phone then putting it back into her black purse.

"I guess we will have to come back, there is no telling when he will be back. Do you want me to take you home or do you need to go back to the station?" Megan asked as she and Robert walked to the glass revolving door of the hotel.

"Could you bring back to the station to get my car?" Robert asked.

Chapter 10
Inside the Mirror

Robert awoke from his sleep. He knew that the woman that he had been dreaming about would be his date and he would be her gift for the night. This Crystal had haunted his dreams and came to him again. He had not dreamed about the other woman, the one with raven hair, for some time. His heart still ached for her. Robert put on his tux and his cape then left the ranch and drove to the Gathering Club.

Robert waited at the door scanning the crowd outside waiting to get into the club. He could see her. He longed for her. He had to be with her.

"My name is Cinder...I mean I am dressed as Cinderella, but my name is Crystal..," before she could give the door man her last name, she was interrupted by Robert.

"My Darling, where have you been? I have been waiting for you," Robert said in a very distinguished tone with a slight accent, like a mix of French and English. She looked at him as he took her hand and escorted her to the door.

"Mr. Towers, you know this young lady?" The doorman asked looking at Robert, who nodded his head. The door man didn't ask any more questions and let them into the club. Crystal followed Robert inside, she thought it looked like a church, with the altar and the row of pews on both sides of the room. A red velvet carpet ran from the door all the way to the altar. She held onto Robert's hand as he led her through the dimly lit room to an open, smoke filled doorway in the back of the altar.

"My name is Robert Towers," Robert said, holding onto Crystal's gloved hand and then giving it a gentle kiss.

"I know, my name is Crystal Stone," she replied, thinking this can't be happening. Robert Towers, the sexiest Rancher in all of Colorado, is escorting her into the club! She thought that he was even sexier in person. She found it hard not to rip off his vampire costume and jump on

him. Robert smiled. They made their way down a dimly lit winding stair case that led down to the bar and club. Crystal could hear dance music and people partying. The room was underground. The walls were painted black and on the walls were lights in the shape of candles. The room was huge. In the middle of the room was a dance floor and stage. A band was playing on the stage, Crystal looked to see who was on stage. It was not Sharron's band. Robert escorted her to a booth with a table. The booth was round and so was the table, the area was roped off by a red velvet rope.

"This is my table. Would you join me Miss Stone?" Robert asked very politely. Crystal could not believe that she was talking to her dream man, but why was he paying so much attention to her? He could have any of these women.

"Robert I would love to, but I have to find my friend and let them know that I am here," Crystal replied as she scanned the room looking for Sharron.

Robert looked at her playfully, then asked, "Is this person of a masculine or feminine gender?"

She looked back at him and then replied, "She is the singer of the headlining band."

Robert smiled back, as Crystal excused herself and walked to the bar to see if she could talk to Sharron.

"What can I get you Darling?" asked the bartender, who was dressed as a sexy cowboy. He was tall. He had a brown cowboy hat on his head, shading his green eyes. He had no shirt and Crystal could see his smooth muscular chest. Sharron had told her about him, and now she could see through his tight fitting faded jeans what Sharron was talking about. Crystal thought back to the night she spent at Sharron's when she was helping her decorate her apartment. Victor came out of the shower and walked out into the living room wearing nothing but a smile.

"Victor, where is Sharron?" Crystal asked, pulling herself back from the memory.

"She is getting ready to get on the stage. I will have her come over on her break," Victor said giving her a Rum and Coke.

"How do you know where I am sitting?" Crystal asked, accepting the drink Victor put in front of her on the bar. He then smiled and winked at her and said in a flirty tone.

"We thought he would be a great early birthday gift for you, happy birthday a day early. Now go back to him before some other woman notices him and takes him away from you. By the way, you look great. I love the Cinderella costume, it is really turning me on," Victor said and then smiled at her as he handed her a drink for Robert.

Sharron was making her way to the stage as Crystal took the bloody Mary with her. Sharron stopped at the bar and gave Crystal a hug and gave Victor a kiss before going on stage.

"Hello, everybody! I am going to sing for you tonight. I would like to start the show off with wishing my best friend Crystal Stone a happy birthday. I hope she enjoys her gift. I would also like to thank the models of Sexiest Ranchers of Colorado Calendar for joining us tonight. Especially, I would like to thank Mr. October himself, Robert Towers. This first song is for my best friend and her date Mr. October, it's called Fairytales. I think it's appropriate for tonight being Halloween and all," Sharron said into the microphone and the crowd cheered and yelled as the band played and she sang. Crystal pushed through the crowd and made her way back to Robert, who was standing waiting for her to return. She smiled as she seated herself back at the table.

"Happy birthday, I am your gift," Robert said as he seated himself next to her in the booth.

"Thank you, you are the sexiest man in the world, and the greatest gift anyone could give me," said Crystal blushing.

"Ah, my dear I am flattered. I am proud to be a guest at your Birthday Ball, Cinderella. Would you like to dance?" He asked her, getting up and bowing to her as he put his hand out for her.

"Robert, I would love to dance, thank you," she replied, then smiled at him. She took his hand and he led her on to the dance floor. Sharron was singing a slow tango like song when they began to dance. Crystal knew that Robert was formerly a ballroom dancer and it showed. He glided her around the dance floor in a lover's tango. She felt light in his embrace and he held her close to his body. He felt hard and muscular against her soft slender body. When he twirled her around and spun her away from him, she felt lost without him to guide her, then he brought her back into his embrace. She felt his body again, she could feel the warmth as it heated her body. She felt his member harden as he pressed himself into her and held her against him. Robert was seducing her on

the dance floor. Crystal felt like he was undressing her with his embrace and she couldn't stop him, all she could do was enjoy the dance. He was taking her and all she could do was allow him to take her right there on the dance floor in front of everyone. When the dance ended Robert had to hold her close to him, because if he didn't they would fall to the floor. He held her until they both regained the control of their trembling bodies then he helped her back to their table.

Mirror

Robert awoke to the sound of the alarm clock beside his bed. He sat up in his bed before getting up for the day.

Chapter 11

Ruth was sitting in the conference room looking at the whiteboard which held the notes and photos of the suspects. The photos and information were in the form of an outline, with two photos of Sharron Jenkins at the top of the board. The first photo was Sharron's mug shot, taken three months before her body was found in City Park. The other photo was Sharron's lifeless body in the Park. Ruth noticed how different the two photos looked. In Sharron's mug shot, she looked like a naive country girl. In the photo of her in the park, she looked like a movie star with her make-up perfectly done and dressed like a model with elegant diamond studs in her ears. Ruth could not understand why this young woman was now dead and they had to find the killer. Ruth thought of her own daughter's photos when she was found. The more she stared at the photo of Sharron's dead body, she didn't see Sharron's face, but her Robin. Ruth remembered that day like it was yesterday....

Robin was a dancer when she got into drugs. She was a smart girl, at least before she moved to Los Angeles. Ruth thought about the day she transferred Robert to LA to find Robin. Robert reported back to her that Robin was doing porno movies and stripping at a club, she was just 18 years old. Ruth remembered the night that Robert called her to come identify her baby girl's body....

Megan and Robert came into the room, interrupting Ruth's thoughts. Ruth wiped away the tears before she turned to face them.

"So, what do we have to add to the evidence board?" Ruth asked when she got her composure back.

"Well, we don't have all that much. When we went to the hotel, Seth Brooks was not there. We will go back and see if we can speak with him later," Megan said as she walked over to the evidence board and looked at it.

"Okay, what do we have so far? Let's try and piece this all together. We have a missing person, Sharron Jenkins, who went missing on June 20th, which was Saturday. The missing person report was called in by her roommate Crystal Stone on Monday June 22nd at 6:00 AM. Then, Tuesday the 23rd of June at six in the morning, a woman's body is found in City Park. Sarah IDs the body to be Sharron Jenkins, our missing person," Megan said looking as the evidence board.

"Yes," Candy said coming into the room and walked up to the evidence board and put up the photo of Sharron and Crystal attaching the photo to a clip on the board.

"Then we have Victor Marshall, the last known person to see Sharron Jenkins alive. We also have Mark Willis, the owner of the Cowboy's Club. He is the employer of Sharron Jenkins, Crystal Stone, and Victor Marshall," Ruth said looking at the report of the suspects.

"We can't forget about Seth Brooks, who was Sharron Jenkins boyfriend, and who is remodeling the Cowboy's Club for Mark Willis," Robert said as he sat next to Megan.

"Did any of you go back and try to speak with Seth Brooks today?" Ruth asked looking at the group.

"I stopped at the Sheraton before coming in, but he had already left. I told the manager to call us when he comes back," JP said coming into the room and going over to his desk.

"Okay, well, we have to wait for that call, then. Let me know when you get it," Ruth said before leaving the room and going back to her office.

"I have to go back home and see how Katie is doing," Megan said.

"What happened to her?" Robert asked.

"Nothing she is just getting old now. She was just a puppy when my parents gave her to me," Megan said shaking her head and thinking that Katie was the only family she had since her parents were killed. Now to think that she might lose Katie made her shudder.

"Would you mind if I stopped by and see her?" Robert asked.

Robert would bring Katie treats ever since he and Megan worked together. He would take Katie out to the park and dog sit her when Megan had to go out of town.

"Yes, you can come over and see her," Megan replied and then smiled at him.

Chapter 12

When Megan and Robert got to Megan's loft, Katie was laying on Megan's bed sleeping. Katie picked her head up and looked at Megan when she came into the bedroom.

"Katie, how are feeling? Did you go out?" Megan asked the sheltie, as she petted Katie's head. Robert came into the bedroom and got down on his knees on the floor next to the bed. He took out a milk bone treat for Katie and she licked his face after he gave her the treat. Robert laughed and gave her another treat that he had in his other hand. He then petted Katie on the head before getting up.

"Looks like she's feeling better, would you like a glass of wine?" Megan asked Robert who was smiling and petting Katie.

"Yeah, that would be great," Robert said following Megan into the living room of the loft then into the kitchen. Megan opened a bottle of wine and went into the cabinet to get to the wine glasses.

"So what do you think about the case?" Megan asked as she placed the crystal wine glasses on the bar.

"I really don't know. I do think that there is more going on at the Cowboy's Club, but I don't know what," Robert said as he poured the wine into one of the glasses and then gave it to Megan who was sitting on a bar stool in front of the counter bar. She waited for Robert to pour a glass of wine for himself before picking up her glass and gently tapping his glass with hers, and then took a sip of the wine. They took the bottle of wine and their glasses with them and went to the overstuffed sofa in the living room to sit and talk.

"I think you are right, there. The Cowboy's club has to have something to do with the murder of Sharron," Megan said, taking another sip of her wine.

"Do you remember the case that we went on a few years ago?"

"Do mean the time when we working as police officers? The first time Ruth made us partners?"

"No, the first case as detectives, the bank robbery."

"Oh yes when we went undercover as a married couple and I became a hostage."

"Yes, the owner of the bank was the brains behind the robbery."

"So you think that Mark Willis could be the murderer or that he had something to do with it?"

"I don't know Meg, but I think we should find out."

"Robert, I've been wanting to know something,"

"What?"

"Why did you ask for the transfer to Los Angeles after the bank robbery case?" Megan asked looking into her wine glass as if she would find the answers there.

Robert thought about how to answer the question knowing that Ruth would never forgive him. He couldn't tell anyone about Ruth's daughter because she wanted it kept quiet.

"Meg, I left because I had to. When you were taken hostage and I blew my cover to save you...I thought that we were getting too involved. That is why I asked Ruth to be transferred," Robert said not really lying, but also not telling the whole truth either.

"Why didn't you say goodbye? When Ruth told me that you were transferred to Los Angeles I was so upset with you. I never thought that I could forgive you. I wanted you to come back because I was falling...but that is here nor there," Megan said then she took another drink of her wine and swallowed hard to keep the tears from forming. Robert didn't know what to say he just took a drink of his wine and sat there. Katie came into the living room and lay down on her faux sheep skin bed that was next to the sofa.

"Meg, I didn't want to leave, but I had to. When you asked me to start a private investigation business with you, I thought we could give us a second chance, but we didn't, we just stayed friends. Maybe that is all we are meant to be," Robert said looking hurt and then forcing a smile. Megan looked up at him but then looked back into the glass of wine.

"So you really think that Mark..," She couldn't finish what she was saying, because Robert leaned over to her and kissed her. Her heart skipped a beat as she kissed him back.

"Meg, you always do this when you start talking about your feelings for me. You always change the subject you never let me know how you feel, and you never allow me to tell you my feelings for you."

"Okay, explain why you left when I needed you?"

"I left after the bank robbery case was solved because you almost got killed. I was falling in love with you Meg. I thought my feelings were getting in the way of us working together."

"If you were falling in love with me then why didn't you tell me? Why didn't you tell me you were leaving?" Megan asked as tears began to roll down her cheek.

"I didn't tell you because we were partners and you always told me that you had no time for a relationship. So how could I tell you that I loved you," Robert said as his eyes filled with tears, but he didn't allow them to fall. Megan looked up at him as a tear rolled down her face. Robert wiped it away from her face with his hand. Then he took her into his arms and kissed her, she fell into his embrace and let herself go. Robert broke the kiss long enough to get off the sofa and pick her up into his arms and carried her into the bedroom. He laid her on the bed and lay next to her and kissed her trembling lips. She could not believe what was happening, but she allowed him to take control. He rolled on top of her trembling body and kissed her lips passionately. They kissed as his hands began to wonder over her body, her brain told her she must stop what was about to happen before it went too far.

"Robert stop...we must stop," she breathed heavily with passion. She didn't want him to stop, but instead for him to make love to her.

Chapter 13
Inside the Mirror

When Megan got to the Gathering Club she knew that she could charm her way into the party.

"Are you on the list?" Asked the doorman dressed as the Mad Hatter.

"I am part of the entertainment," she answered showing him her crystal ball and oracle cards.

"Okay, go on in."

Megan made her way to the party. In the club she saw the dancers on the floor. She made her way over to a table on the side of the dance floor and sat down at the table. She watched Robert and a woman dancing a tango. When the dance ended, she watched him hold the woman in his arms and make their way back to their table. Megan held the pentacle that hung around her neck and watched the couple. She closed her eyes and thought back to when she first came into contact with Robert, it seemed like a lifetime ago...How he seduced her into his bed...She fell for him and was still drawn to him in more ways than one. Watching him seduce this Cinderella was more than she could stand. She took one more look in Robert's direction before making her way to the Ladies room to compose herself.

Megan was splashing water on her face when Crystal entered the Ladies room and made her way into the stall and closed and locked the door. Megan watched and waited until she came back out. She watched as Crystal washed her hands.

"Hi, I saw you on the dance floor, you dance very well," Megan said and then smiled over at Crystal as she dried her hands.

"Thank you," Crystal said then looked into the mirror to apply some lip gloss.

"How long have you known Robert Towers?"

"Not long, but I have admired his calendar photo since it was released."

"I knew him before he became one of Colorado's sexiest Rancher. We were close, but lost touch with each other. I am Megan Sapphire."

"Nice to meet you Megan, I'm Crystal Stone."

Megan and Crystal shook hands.

'I should warn her about Robert,' Megan thought to herself.

"Well I have to get back to my date," Crystal said. As she was about to leave Megan grabbed her arm.

"I believe you could be in danger Crystal."

"What do you mean? What are you talking about?"

"Robert can be dangerous! I know because he was with me. Don't be alone with him. He could hurt you, maybe even kill you," Megan said with a worried look.

"What the fuck are you talking about?" Crystal yelled as she pulled her arm out of Megan's grasp, and opened the door and left.

"Hello Megan. It has been a long time," Robert said as he came into the Ladies room, closing and locking the door behind him.

"So we meet again, Robert," Megan said as she held the old Ritual dagger behind her back so he couldn't see it. She trembled as her mind wondered for a moment...I need to do this...I can't bring myself to do this.

Megan looked up at Robert as he stood in front of her, with a cunning smile on his face. He looked like a fox charming his prey before he ate it, and she was his prey.

"Megan I have missed you," Robert said in a tender voice. He knew that there was more to this meeting and he had to charm her. He moved toward her until he spotted the dagger she held in her hand.

"What are you doing Megan?"

"I have to this Robert. I have to stop you. My heart is being torn."

Robert backed away from Megan just in time, as she lunged with the dagger aiming for his chest, but missing him. He grabbed her arm before she could lunge for him again. He pushed her away, knocking her to the floor. She banged her head and was knocked unconscious. The dagger fell out of her hand beside her. Robert tried to pick up the dagger but it burned his hand.

"What a clever little witch. Putting a spell on that cursed thing so I can't touch it," Robert said as he dropped the dagger then looked at the burn on the palm of his hand.

"Megan, my Darling, we could have been so good together. If we could just come to an understanding...that to have me..," Robert was cut off by the sound of someone trying to get into the room. He left Megan lying on the floor as he went through the other door that led to a hall.

Mirror

Robert woke up and looked down at Megan who was lying beside him with her head on his chest. He could feel himself getting aroused again and knew he could not make love to the sleeping angel. He decided it would be better to go sleep on the sofa. He saw that they were both fully clothed so he knew nothing happened. He wondered why Megan stopped him from making love to her. He gently moved her head off his chest onto the pillow as he got up off of the bed. Megan rolled over onto her side of the bed. Robert left the room and went to the sofa and went back to sleep.

Chapter 14
Inside the Mirror

"So Crystal, what do you say we leave? I would like to go for a walk, the air is a bit stuffy in here," Robert said hoping that she would say yes so he could get to know her in a more intimate way.

"Yes. I think it would be nice to go out and get some fresh air," Crystal said getting up and then they walked arm and arm with him through the crowd and out the exit.

When they got outside Crystal noticed the air was cool but not cold. She looked up at the full moon. It was so close the she could reach out and touch it. Robert looked at the moon then at Crystal.

"I would like to get know you Crystal. Shall we take a stroll?"

"Yes, of course, Robert. I would like to get to know you, also."

They walked in silence. Crystal could not believe that she was walking down the sidewalk holding hands with Robert Towers.

"This may sound corny, but I look at your picture every day," she shyly confessed.

"Why, Miss Stone, I am flattered," Robert said, then with a smile he put his hand over his heart in a show of gratitude.

"I also read your article in the newspaper."

"What did you think?" Robert asked as they stopped at a bus stop bench and sat down.

"I thought it was great, and strange, but cute that you have a pet piglet named Ginger,"

"Ginger is my prize piglet, she even stays in the house at night," Robert said and then laughed as he looked at Crystal who looked like she was listening to every word. She didn't care what he was talking about. She just enjoyed being next to him and enjoyed the scent of him. She wondered what the scent was. She tried to guess what the scent was but couldn't guess. All she knew was that it was intoxicating.

"What is the scent of your cologne?" Crystal asked interrupting what he was saying. It didn't matter to her she was not listening anyway.

"I am not wearing any cologne. What you smell my dear is my natural scent," Robert said as he leaned over so she could sniff his face and neck.

"Crystal, can I take you home?" He asked as he felt her breath on his neck. He could sense that she was entrapped in his scent.

"Well, I just live down the street. We could go to my apartment," she said.

"Is it close or should we get a cab?" Robert asked as he stood up and then helped Crystal to her feet. When she was standing beside him, she took out her cell phone out of her purse and called a cab.

When Robert and Crystal entered the house he looked at her with lust in his eyes.

"Crystal I want to kiss you. I can't wait any longer," Robert said taking her into his strong arms. He pushed her onto the sofa and lay on top of her and kissed her passionately. He kissed slowly down to her neck.

"Crystal I want you," he said softly as he got up and picked her up off the sofa into his arms.

"Let's go to the bedroom," Crystal whispered, trapped under his spell. He kissed her tenderly as he carried her from the living room down the hall to the bedroom. He walked into the bedroom and laid her on the bed and then looked down at her. He couldn't believe how much he wanted to take her. He lay down next to her and kissed her passionately. She rolled on top of him and kissed him as she ripped at his white dress shirt. It opened and then she licked his smooth chest. She then slowly moved down, kissing all the way down to the waist band of his dress pants. He rolled her back on to the bed and lay on top of her now trembling body. He pushed his hard body against her so she was trapped between his body and the mattress. Crystal looked into Robert's eyes and she could see herself flying in ecstasy with him. He held Crystal, who was entrapped by ecstasy, want, and need for him to take her body.

"Take me Robert, Take me now!" She screamed out.

Robert ripped at the top of the Cinderella costume until her breasts broke free of their prison. He lifted the bottom of the gown and found that she was ready for him. Robert broke away from the lust just long enough to undo his pants and take them off. Then he lay back on top of her pushing himself into her and taking her to a pleasure she never knew existed. Crystal cried out in pleasure as Robert nestled his mouth into the soft flesh of her shoulders next to her neck. He gently nipped at her neck as he slowly made love to her.

"Take me now!" Crystal screamed out.

Robert willingly obeyed. He looked up at her and then looked up at the ceiling as his eyes turned black. He bared his sharp, long fangs then brought his mouth to her soft neck. Crystal cried out as he nestled his mouth into her neck and bit her. She softly cried out in passion as he pushed his member deeper and harder into her. He let out a whimper like a pup wanting to be fed. As soon as he got the first drop of her warm, sweet blood in his mouth he spilled his seed into her. He pushed into her again as he took more of Crystal's life fluid, he drank and fed like a suckling infant on his mother's tit. He stopped feeding and he felt her get weak, he heard her heartbeat pound in his ears. He rolled off of her body as he looked at her eyes they were glossy and her skin was pale white, she laid on the bed, not moving. He put his ear up to her nose and listened to see if she was breathing. He felt her breath, but it was weak. Robert left the room and closed the door to the room and left her alone. He left Crystal's house, taking her key with him.

Mirror

Megan awoke and reached for Robert, but he was not there. She got up when she heard the sound of Robert moaning from the living room. She went into the living room and found him sleeping on the sofa. Megan went back into the bedroom and took the blanket off the chair in the corner by the window. She took the blanket back to the living room and covered Robert with it and then kissed him and went back to her bed and went to sleep.

Chapter 15
Inside the Mirror

Megan awoke and found herself lying on the cold Ladies room floor.
"Are you OK?" asked a young woman dressed as a cat.
"Yeah, I'm fine. Just drank a bit too much," Megan answered quickly.
Megan got up and picked up the ritual dagger. The dagger was a stiletto. It would go through anything and pierce the heart. She looked into the mirror and then left the restroom and the club.
She knew that she had to find more information about vampires and their way of life. She remembered a club on Colfax called the Dungeon Club, an underground club for people with dark fetishes. She decided that she might find all she needed to know there.

Megan entered the Dungeon Club and went to the bar to get a drink.
"What will it be, honey?" the bartender asked. Megan thought she looked like she stepped out of a vampire movie. Her skin was a pale white, her eyes bloodshot, and when she smiled, Megan noticed her sharp fangs.
"I'll have a bloody Mary."
"Here enjoy, that will be $4.00," She said as she handed Megan her drink. Megan paid and then turned to face the dance floor, she watched the dancers. They looked like they were possessed. People pulled their slaves on chains as they went through an entryway with a wooden sign that hung over the doorway that read 'To the Caverns'. She followed them to find out where they were going. Megan went through the entryway and found a black iron stair case winding down into the dark. She went down the stairs to the caverns.
When she reached the bottom of the stairs, there was a cage with bars around it. Megan noticed the man inside the cage was dressed in a dark brown monk's robe. The man had a scar on his face that went from the right side of his forehead down across to the left side of his neck. He handed Megan a number and then pointed at the torch on the wall and then turned to face the staircase.
She took a torch from the wall and walked down the dark hall to the deep caverns. She walked until she came to a big round room that was

dark except for the glow of her torch. She felt the fear of the unknown. She faced fear before and knew that she could let the fear go. As she relaxed, she looked around the room, it was dark and hard to see. She closed her eyes so she could sense everything and take it all in. She heard moaning and screaming. She felt the eroticism and the lust; also the fear that was coming from the caverns. Megan opened her eyes and walked down one of the dark halls, the heels of her boots clicking on the stone floor.

She heard moaning and crying. She saw a blue light up ahead of her. She walked towards the light. The light led her to a room. She looked in the room, there was an altar in the middle of the room. A woman was lying on the altar. Megan thought she looked like an angel. She was dressed in a long see-through gown with a shirtless man kneeling in front of her. She was laying there moaning in ecstasy while the man licked the blood off of her nipple that slowly flowed from a small bite mark on her breast. Megan watched the couple in their erotic moment until the man looked back and saw her watching them. He hissed at Megan and bared his sharp fangs. She took the hint and left the room and walked down the hall until she was back in the round room. Megan saw a young man in his twenties enter the room. He was followed by a young woman who was on a chain which the man in front was holding. The man looked at Megan as he passed, his black hair was cut in a shag cut. His eyes were brown with a touch of gold in them. She noticed that his face was pale and white as snow and his lips where a deep red and full. She watched him glide past her like he was floating on the air. She thought that this man looked sexy, the way that he wore his ripped jeans and leather jacket. Megan felt this man was dangerous. She felt his gaze burn into her soul when he looked at her as he past. The young woman had blonde hair that was cut into a bob style. She was thin and was wearing a short black skirt and white see - through blouse. Megan noticed that the woman had a hard time keeping up with her master because of her five inch high heels. Every time her master pulled on the chain she fell to the stone floor. When she would fall, she would just push herself back up and look at Megan. She noticed the woman's eyes filled up with tears and her blonde bangs kept falling down across her face as she pulled herself back up again. Megan thought the woman looked like Jesus walking on the road with the cross, her knees were all bloody and her body broken *and bruised. Megan knew that this couple was the one that she was waiting for. As the woman passed and disappeared into a hall, Megan followed them down the hall into the cavern. They entered a room lit with a red light. She watched the man thread the chain into big iron hooks. He took a padlock and locked the end of the chain to one of the links.*

"What do you want?" the man yelled, looking back to find Megan standing at the entrance of the room.

"I have come to watch the show," Megan replied with an evil laugh.

"So you come for free food have you?"

"No, you just sparked my interest. You intrigued me the way that you're taking command of the woman. I would like watch how you take her...I am looking for some entertainment," Megan said as she walked over to the chained woman and gently brushed a tear away from the woman's cheek with the tip of her finger.

The man laughed an evil laugh and turned his attention to the two women. He then walked over and grabbed Megan and kissed her, as the blonde woman watched. He then turned to the blonde woman and grabbed the front of her blouse and ripped the sheer fabric from her body. Megan turned toward the woman and watched him lick her nipples while he rubbed his crotch. Megan knew what the man wanted and that he was going to get it soon. He looked up at her as he pushed his body hard into the woman. He then laughed and turned to his slave who was crying. He gently touched her face and brushed the tears away. He then looked at Megan with lust in his eyes. Megan looked at him and felt for the dagger that she had tucked into the back of her dress. She pulled the dagger out of its holder and held it behind her back, ready to use it.

"I think I am going to have you first, you hot bitch. I know you want me also. What is your name sweet, woman? My name is Seth," Seth said in a cunning tone as he at her with hunger in his eyes.

"What did you have in mind, Seth?" Megan asked.

"Do you want to play, my dear?" Seth asked as he made his way to Megan, who was ready for him if he tried to bite her. He softly touched her face and pushed her up against the wall as he kissed her. He pushed himself hard up against her. She could feel him getting aroused as he rubbed himself up against her.

"You stay right there," he said and then he released one of the blonde woman's hands without moving away from Megan. He took the

woman's wrist and bit the tender flesh, the woman did not scream or yell. Megan remembered reading in her spell book about people being kidnapped or willingly becoming food for a vampire or a vampiress. Megan looked at the woman as tears rolled down her face as the vampire fed on her. After Seth was done having his snack he turned his attention back to Megan. Megan grabbed his crotch and rubbed it as she slipped the dagger into the belt of her dress. She then undid his jeans and slipped her hand inside and touched him.

"So you want me, do you?" Seth pushed himself against her hand. He then pulled her away from the stone wall and guided her to the cold stone floor with him.

"I'm going to take you now," Seth said as he kneeled between Megan's open legs pulling down his jeans. She took the dagger out of its hiding place and held it behind her back, between her and the floor. Seth leaned down and kissed her, hard, as he tore at the front of her leather dress, trying to undo the front clasps at the top that caged her ample breasts.

"I'm going to fuck you now," Seth said as he was about to enter her.

"I don't think so," Megan said angrily, and showing him the dagger.

"What the fuck is this?" Seth yelled bearing his sharp fangs at her.

"I'm going to kill you, asshole!" Megan yelled trying to make the vampire use his charm on her.

The vampire leaned in to bite her showing his bloody fangs from his last feeding. Megan held the dagger up to him and plunged the point into his chest piercing his heart.

She began to chant the magic words
"I resist the creatures of the night,
I resist to bleed for you!
I resist the fear you give,
I resist for you to take me!
I take you!"

Megan chanted the words again and then again on the third time she pushed the dagger blade deep into his heart. Seth screamed and tried to pull the dagger out but he couldn't touch it because it burned his hands. Megan rolled Seth off of her as he hit the stone floor blood gushed out of his body. The chained woman screamed.

Megan rushed to her and put her hand over her mouth to stifle the sounds. The two women watched as the vampire's body turned old right in front of them. All the time Seth clawed at the dagger trying to remove it. When he found that he could not pull the dagger out of his chest, he started to rip at his own skin. He tore his own flesh off his bones. He struggled until his body gave out and he began to turn to ash.

Megan unchained the woman, who was crying and shaking and she tried to run out of the room.

Mirror

Megan awoke to the sound of the ringing of her phone.

"Hello?" she said in a sleepy voice.

"Hello, is Cindy there?" asked a man's voice.

"No, you must have the wrong number," Megan answered and then she hung up the phone, and then rolled over and went back to sleep.

Chapter 16

Robert opened his eyes when the phone rang. He listened to the conversation before going back to sleep.

Inside the Mirror

It took two days for Crystal to wake. Robert saw that she was shivering. He knew that her body would be weak. He put his hand on her, she felt like she was on fire as she shivered and sweat at the same time. She stared to cough and then she coughed again. Robert felt heat on the side of her neck when he touched her, and she winced in pain at his touch.

The day slowly slipped away as Robert watched the woman sleep in her Cinderella costume. Her breathing was shallow as her body burned up with fever. The day turned to afternoon, afternoon turned into evening. She screamed in pain and ripped at her gown trying to stop the pain. Her body convulsed like she was being possessed by a demon in some late night exorcism movie. When the pain subsided, she relaxed and went back to sleep.

Robert softly put his hand on Crystal's forehead, she felt like she was burning up with fever. He felt to see if she had a pulse, she did, but he could tell that it was very weak. He also noticed that her breathing was very shallow. He lay down on the bed and held the fragile woman in his arms to comfort her.

Crystal thought she was dreaming when she heard Robert softly whisper.

"It won't be long now my dear. Just go with it, and let it take you."

Crystal opened her eyes and looked up at him then she closed them again. Robert kissed her now blue lips tenderly. He lifted her top lip with his finger and saw the sharp fangs were starting to form. He sat with the woman a moment longer before he felt that he should leave her alone to go through the rest of the rebirth.

After Robert left the room, he stood beside the door and could hear her screaming. He could feel her pain because he had gone through the same kind of pain so long ago when he turned...

The Queen of the land had taken a liking to him and wanted him for her lover. One night as he slept, she came to him.

"Sir Robert, I know that you were my husband's brother, so that makes you the only one to keep the king's bloodline going. We must do this and you must help me rule the kingdom," Queen Val Dior said as she got into his bed.

Robert took the queen into his arms and entered he. That is when it happened, when they took each other...

When he awoke, he felt pain like his body was splitting into and his skin was tearing off of his body. He could feel his blood boiling and his heart burning like it was on fire. He felt the pain like someone was piercing his heart with a sword in battle. He felt alone and scared until he heard a voice.

"You are now mine, my king,"

Robert felt pain again and the loving hands that held him as he finished with the agonizing pain of his rebirth...

Robert heard a crash and he opened Crystal's bedroom door and found her on the floor covered with the beige velvet curtains.

"Crystal, can you hear me?" Robert asked knowing that what she felt now was the pain of hunger.

Crystal awoke as Robert helped her to her feet and they walked out onto the balcony. She looked out into the darkness of the night.

"Crystal, don't panic, you have to eat now," Robert said as he took her into his arms and they jumped off of the balcony and flew into the dark night sky.

"Crystal do you feel my love inside of you? Do you trust me?" Robert asked softly as he held her fragile, weak body closer to him.

"Yes I do my love," Crystal replied and then she fainted.

Mirror

Robert awoke sweating. He sat up, stretched and then yawned as he got up. Then, he let Katie outside as he went to the kitchen to make coffee. He took Megan's keys off of the key hook by the door and left.

Chapter 17

Megan was awoken by the by the alarm going off. She really didn't want to get up, she wanted to go back to sleep.

"I guess I better get up, there is a case that still needs solving," Megan said to herself as she got off the bed. She smelled the coffee brewing in the kitchen. She wondered who put on the pot. Then she remembered Robert had slept over, he must have started the coffee. She undressed so that she could take a shower before starting her day.

"Meg, are you awake?" Robert called as he came to the bedroom and found Megan naked heading to the bathroom. Megan grabbed for her silk robe to cover herself, but it was too late, he saw her. He just stood in the entryway and took in the beauty of the naked woman putting on her robe. When he got his composure back he didn't know what to say.

"I brought donuts," he said, blushing and then leaving the room so that Megan could put on her robe.

"Robert could you please pour me a cup of coffee?" Megan said as she tied her robe closed then shook her head as she went out into the living room and sat down on the sofa.

"What kind of donut would you like?" Robert asked coming into the living area from the kitchen.

"What kind did you get?" Megan asked, blushing and then laughing at the sight of Robert standing with his mouth open, like a teenager seeing a naked girl for the first time.

"I am sorry that I..," Robert started to explain but was stopped by Megan as she got up and walked over to him and kissed him. They deepened the kiss as he untied her robe and she pulled his tee-shirt over his head. Before the lovers could get too far Megan's cell phone rang.

"Robert, I have to answer the phone, it's probably Ruth," Megan said pulling away to grab the phone off of the coffee table, while Robert kept kissing her neck and embracing her body.

"Hello," Megan said into her phone.

"Megan? It is Ruth, we have a situation. I need you and Robert and meet me at the Sheraton hotel."

Chapter 18

When Megan and Robert got to the Sheraton Hotel, they were met by police cars blocking the entrance to the parking garage.

"There is no parking!" called a police officer walking over to Megan's car.

"Oh, I'm sorry Detective Sapphire, the Sergeant is waiting for you on the top floor," the officer said when he saw Megan and Robert.

When they got to the top floor Megan pulled her car into a parking space. They saw Ruth and Sarah standing by a burned up Cadillac. Ruth walked over to them when they got out of the car.

"What do we have here?" Megan asked.

"What we have here is what is left of Seth Brook's rental car. What we could find out so far from the valet is that, Seth Brooks got into his car and it exploded," Ruth said as the trio walked over to the burnt up car.

"Robert, why don't you go and find out what you can from the valet," Megan said.

"Ok," he said leaving her and Ruth to investigate the car.

"So what caused the explosion?" Megan asked.

"We don't know, but forensics thinks that it could have been gasoline. They are running tests on the ashes now. If it was caused by gasoline then we might have an accident," Ruth said.

"Well, I am done here. I'm going to take what is left of the body back to the lab. I will let you know what I find," Sarah said standing up as she removed her surgical gloves.

"I think I am going to check out Mr. Brooks' room. We were planning on talking to him this morning before going to the station," Megan said.

When Megan got to the lobby of the hotel, she walked up to the front desk to get the key to Seth's room.

"Hi, I am Detective Megan Sapphire and I would like the key to room one twenty on the eleventh floor, please. Seth Brooks' room."

"I will get the key for you, Detective," said the woman behind the desk.

"Thank you. Could you inform the maid not to make up the room? I want to see it exactly as Mr. Brooks left it," Megan said and then went to the elevator.

Megan got off the elevator on the eleventh floor and walked to room 120. She unlocked the door and went inside. As she looked around, she noticed the unmade king size bed that faced a dresser with a television. In the corner of the room was a desk with a lamp and laptop. She went over to the desk and turned on the laptop. 'I hope this doesn't ask for a password.' To her dismay, when the screen came on a password box showed on the screen. She turned off the laptop. She walked over to the closet to see what she could find. She found two pairs of blue jeans, a couple of tee-shirts, a pair of black dress pants, and a dark blue suit. On the shelves, she found a pair of sneakers and a pair of black leather dress shoes. Megan took out the suitcase that was resting on floor of the closet and carried it to the bed and opened it. Inside were some men's boxer shorts, some rolled up socks, and an address book. She took out the address book and looked through it. In it she found Crystal Stone's address and phone number. Megan took the address book and put it with the laptop so she could start an evidence pile. She went back to the bed and looked through the nightstand. 'Why would someone want to kill you, Seth' She discovered Seth's wallet. The wallet was pretty bare, inside was an American Express card and Seth's driver's license.

"That's strange, why didn't Seth have his wallet or his license if he was going out for a drive?"

She put the wallet with the other clues, and then she went into the bathroom. Megan looked at the towels laying on the floor and Seth's razor on the vanity. She went back to the pile of evidence on the desk and noticed the hotel phone, the message light was blinking. She picked up the receiver to listen to the message.

"You have one message," said a recording. Megan waited for the beep and then listened to the message.

"Mr. Brooks you have a message at the front desk," Megan hung up the phone and then looked around the room one last time just in case she missed something. When she was satisfied she went to the door and left the room and closed the door behind her.

Megan walked back to the elevator to go down to the front desk. When the doors opened, Robert was getting off the elevator.

"Well, fancy meeting you here," Robert said when he saw her standing in front of him.

"How did you know I was up here?" Megan asked as she made her way into the elevator pushing him back inside with her.

"Ruth told me that you were up here to see what you could find in Seth's room. Did you find anything?"

"Yes, I found a laptop with a password protection, his wallet, an address book, and a message from the front desk."

"The message was about an envelope left at the valet booth this morning. The valet said that it was found sitting on the desk when he returned from checking the parking garage. He said that it had Seth Brook's name and room number on the front of the envelope. The valet gave it to the front desk," Robert said.

"Did anyone see who put the envelope on the desk?" Megan asked when the doors opened to the elevator and they stepped out into the lobby.

"No. It was early this morning, around four am. The valet said that he was just starting his shift. He said no one was at the desk," Robert said looking down at the note pad that he held in his hand.

Megan felt like she just hit a big brick wall in the case. Their only lead to the case was a dead end.

"Hello," Megan said as she walked over to the front desk.

"Hello, Detective Sapphire. What can I do for you?" The woman at the front desk asked.

"I was wondering what time Seth Brooks came to the desk to pick up the envelope that was left for him?"

"I was not here, but I will check and see if the night shift made a note of that," the woman said as she looked through the computer and then at the clipboard hung on the wall in back of her.

"I don't see anything here, just that she left a message for Mr. Brooks this morning at six o' clock," the woman said as she turned back to Robert and Megan.

"Thank you," Megan said.

She and Robert walked over to the door that led to the valet desk outside. They were met by Ruth, Candice, and JP who were standing at the valet desk.

"Megan what did you find in Seth's room?" Ruth asked.

"I found Seth's laptop but it's protected by a password. I found his wallet with his driver's license, which I thought was strange if he was going to drive his car..," Megan answered Ruth.

"That doesn't make any sense. His driver's license was not with him? Then he must have gone to his car for something else. Who knew that Seth was staying here, and that he had a car in the garage?" Ruth asked looking at everyone waiting for one of them to answer her question.

"I know that Crystal Stone knew, because she told us that he was staying here," JP said looking at his notepad that held his notes about the case.

"Why don't you go bring in Crystal Stone for questioning? Don't let on about Seth Brooks being dead," Ruth said to Candice and JP.

"Ok," Candice said and then she and JP left.

"Megan you and Robert go check out the surveillance tapes and find out who left the envelope for Seth. When you are done meet me at the station and we will go from there," Ruth said.

Chapter 19

Candice and JP arrived at Crystal Stone's house. Candice was the first one to reach the door. She knocked, but there was no answer. She took out her cell phone and called Crystal's phone but there was no answer, all she got was her voicemail. She had to ask Crystal some questions.

"Maybe she is still at work, Candy," JP said when he run up to the door and stopped in front of her.

"Yeah, maybe we should go there," she replied.

As they were about to leave they saw a black limo pull up in front of the house and the chauffer opened the back door and helped Crystal out of the car. Candice and JP watched as she leaned back into the car then she got back out and stood beside the open car door.

"Thank you, it was fun. Tell your friend that I will be waiting for his call and the extra check," Crystal said to the person in the car. Candice and JP could not see who was in the back of the car. Crystal turned to face the house. She was startled to find Candice and JP waiting for her on the porch.

"Detectives, what is wrong? What are you doing here?" Crystal asked.

"Crystal Stone, we would like you to come to the station with us if you don't mind. We would like to ask you some questions," Candice said as she walked over to Crystal and escorted her over to her Jeep and helped Crystal in the back seat.

"What's the meaning of this?" Crystal asked.

"Miss Stone, we are not arresting you, we just need to take you to the station to ask you some questions," JP said.

"Ask me questions? About what?" Crystal asked.

"Where were you last night and this morning?" JP asked looking back at Crystal.

"I was out with a friend," she replied.

"What's that friend's name?"

"I think I would like my lawyer," Crystal said.

No one said another word until they got to the police station.

"Crystal Stone, I am going to read you your Miranda Warnings. You have right to remain silent. Anything you say can and will be used against you in a court of law. You have the right to an attorney. If you cannot afford an attorney, one will be provided for you. Do you understand the rights I just read to you?" Candice asked looking at Crystal who was sitting in the chair across from her.

"I would like to call my lawyer," Crystal said.

Candice pushed the black desk phone over in front of her so she could make the call.

Crystal just finished dialing when there was a knock on the integration room door. Candy got up and opened the door to. Ruth was standing in front of the door. Candy closed the door and went out into the hall with Ruth.

"Did she say anything about Seth's murder?" Ruth asked.

"She hasn't said anything. She is calling her lawyer," Candy said.

"You didn't say anything about Seth being dead when you brought her in did you?"

"No, we just said that we needed to ask her some questions."

"Ok, let's not say anything about it yet. Let's just question her about her whereabouts and tell her that Seth has gone missing."

"Alright, maybe she will tell us more."

"Ok, well, let's do this then," Ruth said opening the door to the integration room.

"Hello, Miss Stone. I am Sergeant Ruth Toshibalua. I am going to sit in while you are being questioned," Ruth said extending her hand to Crystal as a greeting. Crystal shook hands with Ruth and then Ruth sat down in the chair that JP was sitting in after he got up to get another chair in the corner of the room.

"Miss Stone, would you like to begin, or would you rather wait for your lawyer?" Candice asked as she sat back down in her chair.

"I have nothing to hide, but I would rather wait for my attorney, if you don't mind," Crystal answered.

"Miss Stone would you like anything while we wait? Coffee, a pop, water, or tea?" JP asked playing the nice cop role.

"A coffee with cream and two sugars would be nice, thank you," Crystal replied with politeness.

"Candice, Sarge, would either of you like anything?" JP asked before leaving the room to get the coffee.

"Yeah coffee would be great thanks," Candice said.

"Nothing for me, but thank you for asking, JP," Ruth replied.

JP opened the door to leave and go get the coffees. When he was about to close the door behind him, a man came to the door.

"I am Crystal Stone's lawyer. Are you the questioning officer?" the overweight man in a dark business suit asked. "Fortunately for her, I was at the station with another client."

"Miss Stone is being questioned in here," JP said opening the door wider so the man could go into the room. He went in the room and looked at Crystal then he gave a vague glance at Candice and Ruth before saying anything. Candice got the lawyer a chair and put it next to the one that Crystal was sitting in. When the man was seated he opened up his briefcase and took out a yellow legal pad and pen. When he was satisfied with his surroundings and his writing tools he introduced himself.

"I am Mr. Carpenter, senior lawyer at Carpenter and McEntire law firm. I will be representing Miss Stone. I was hired by the Cowboy's Club and Miss Stone's employer, Mark Willis," Mr. Carpenter said, before writing on the pad of paper that was in front of him. Candice read what was on the paper it said 'Questioning Crystal Stone by...'

"My name is Detective Candice Carmon and this here is Sergeant Ruth Toshibalua," Candice said.

Taking care, Mr. Carpenter wrote Candice's and Ruth's names on the paper. As Candy watched, JP came back with the coffees and a pop for himself. After giving Candy and Crystal their coffees, he realized that he hadn't asked the lawyer if he wanted something to drink.

"I am sorry, would you like something to drink?" JP asked Mr. Carpenter who was busy writing his notes.

"No thank you, I am fine, and your name is?" Mr. Carpenter asked without looking up from his pad of paper.

"I am Detective John Paul," JP said as he sat down and opened his can of cola. When he pulled the tab on the can there was a hissing sound and then a pop that came from the can.

Candice took a sip of her coffee before setting it down on the table. She took out a hand held recorder, and placed it on the table in front of Crystal after pressing the record button.

"Miss Stone where were you last night and this morning?" Candice asked. Candice looked at Crystal then at Mr. Carpenter as he wrote the question on the pad, as if he was in school writing notes in class. When he was done he looked at Crystal and said.

"Crystal you can answer that."

"I was out at a party last night. I didn't get home until today, when you saw me get out of the limo," Crystal replied taking a sip of her coffee.

"Miss Stone, do you have anyone that can verify to that?"

"No, I don't. I can't get these people involved," Crystal said looking at her lawyer.

"And why can't you tell us who you were with?" Candice asked wrinkling her forehead with a look of confusion.

"Because I can't...because it is the Cowboy's Club policy that we do not give out anyone's identity," Crystal said looking at her lawyer for help.

"So it was not just a party, it was business then. You were working at this party?" Candice asked.

"Detective, I think my client answered your question. May we move on now?" Mr. Carpenter asked coming to Crystal's rescue. He knew the policy himself because he wrote it when the club opened.

Reluctantly Candice went on with her questioning.

"Miss Stone when was the last time you saw or spoke to Seth Brooks?" Candice asked watching the way that Crystal reacted to the question.

"He called me last week, looking for Sharron and I took the message," Crystal replied showing no sign that she was lying or telling the truth, she just sat there looking at Candice.

"Crystal, do you know if Sharron Jenkins went to see Seth Brooks at any time before she was killed?" Ruth asked.

"No...I mean I don't think so... but she could have. I didn't hang out with Sharron all that much, we just shared a house together," Crystal said.

Mr. Carpenter finished with his notes and then clicked his pen closed.

"I think that my client answered all of your questions. We will be going now, or are you going to detain my client any further?" Mr. Carpenter asked picking up his briefcase and putting his pad of paper and pen back inside. He then shook hands with everyone but Crystal who he helped out of her chair and then headed for the door.

Ruth, Candice, and JP waited until Crystal and her lawyer left the room and shut the door, before making plans to go further with the investigation.

"What we need to do is find out where Crystal was and what she was doing. I think that we need to see if Mark Willis can tell us who she was with last night and this morning," Candice said as the trio left the integration room.

"I don't think that we need to ask Mark Willis yet. I think we should keep an eye on Crystal and see what we can find out," Ruth said as she left Candice and JP to lock up the room.

Chapter 20

Megan looked at the surveillance tape of last night. She watched the valet lock up the car keys in the safe then leave the desk and go into the hotel. She waited for him to return but all she saw was the empty valet desk. She stared at the monitor looking at the empty area around the desk and the hotel door. She then watched the clock tick. It was eleven at night when the valet left the desk. She then saw people walk by the desk at midnight. She viewed men and women that were dressed up like they were going to a night club. She watched for what felt like an hour of people leaving the hotel.

"I haven't found anything yet. How about you, Robert? Did you find anything that could give us a clue as to who might have left the envelope at the valet desk?" Megan asked as she put her tape on pause. She got up from the desk and walked to the back of the room to stretch her legs. In the back of the room she found a long table with a coffee pot and mini fridge. She opened the fridge and found it filled with food for them. She took out a sandwich wrapped in saran wrap and labeled "ham and cheese".

"I am having some coffee and a sandwich. Would you like anything?" Megan asked Robert who was still looking at his monitor.

"Yeah, I could us a break right about now. My eyes are getting dry from looking at this monitor," Robert said as he got up out of his chair. He rubbed his stinging eyes as he walked over to her.

"Do you want some coffee?" Megan asked as she poured some coffee into a paper cup.

"This is going to take some time, so I was thinking maybe we should view the tapes together one at a time. If we do that maybe I will catch something that you missed and you can see what I missed," Robert said taking the paper cup that she passed to him.

"We can do that if we don't find anything on our own. I think that the time would go faster if we look at our own tapes first," Megan said and then smiled knowing that Robert just wanted to sit next to her. It made her feel like a cute school girl and the cute boy wanted to sit next to her in class. Megan went back to her desk, leaving Robert standing at the table drinking his coffee. She turned the tape back on and watched for what seemed forever. She glanced at the time on the tape, it was two in the morning when she saw a group of men and women walk by the valet desk and then go into the hotel. She noticed that they were dressed like they just came back from a night on the town. Then there was nothing for an hour, until she saw a woman dressed in a long dress. She had on a head scarf that covered her face. Megan watched as the woman walked up to the valet desk and then looked around before taking something out of her bag. Megan leaned in closer to the monitor to get a better look. The woman held something in her hand that looked like an envelope. She looked around her to see if anyone was coming and then placed the envelope on the valet desk, and then walked away and out of the surveillance camera's view.

"I think I found what we are looking for," Megan said rewinding the tape and playing it back so Robert could view it also. After the tape was rewound to the part she was looking for she pressed play to watch it again. They replayed the tape about three times to make sure that it was an envelope that the woman placed on the desk.

"The only problem with this clue is that our suspect is covered from head to toe. What we see of her skin is her hand and wrist. We can't even see her eyes," Robert said as they viewed the tape for the third time.

Megan stopped the tape and studied the woman on the tape for her height, her weight, and her build. She even studied the way the woman walked. She was not sure who this woman could be. She did know that there were only two woman that she knew that knew Seth Brooks was staying at the hotel. That was Sharron Jenkins who was dead and Crystal Stone as far as they knew. Megan stopped the tape and took it out of the viewing machine.

"We need to show this to Ruth and see if we can get more information

Chapter 21

Megan and Robert rushed into Ruth's office without knocking on the door.

"Ruth I think we have found something, you need to watch this," Megan said.

"What did you find?" Ruth asked looking at them in surprise.

"We need a VCR and a television," Megan said, leaving the office to get the items that she needed. When she came back JP was behind her wheeling in the television cart from the officers break lounge. Megan allowed JP to set up the viewing screen and tape.

"It is right here, watch, there is a woman on this tape," Megan said as Ruth got up out of her chair and sat on the edge of her desk to get a better view of the television.

"Who is that?" Ruth asked when she saw the woman dressed in a head scarf on the screen.

"I don't know, maybe we can have this part of the tape enlarged and get a better look at her," JP said.

"Do you know of someone that can do that?" Megan asked.

"I do. Take it down stairs and give the tape to Kathy Hayward, and tell her I need this part of the tape enlarged to see the woman better," Ruth told JP who took the tape with him as he left.

"Megan what do you think? Do you have any thought about who this woman is?" Ruth asked returning to her chair behind her desk.

"No, but I think we should watch Crystal Stone."

"I agree. Why don't you and Robert do a stakeout on the street in front her house? I will have Candice stakeout the street on the side of the house, so we have the house surrounded. Meanwhile, I am going to take a look at the photos that were taken at the garage that forensics sent over," Ruth said before Megan and Robert left.

When they got to the house, Megan parked across the street from Crystal's house. They could see the front porch from where she was parked. Megan saw Candy drive by and turn on the side street. Megan watched Crystal's house but she didn't see anything unusual. She thought to herself 'We don't even know what we are looking for? Our only lead was that Crystal knew where Seth Brooks was staying.'

"Can I ask you question, Meg?" Robert asked looking at Crystal's Victorian house.

"Yeah, what?" Megan asked without looking at him.

"Why did you stop what was going on between us last night?"

"What do you mean?"

"What do you mean, what do I mean?"

"Robert, we can't do this...we can't go back...I can't take you leaving..," Megan said in a shaky voice as tears were beginning to form in her eyes, she just blinked them back to keep them from falling.

Before she could finish Robert's cell phone rang.

"Hello, this is Robert Towers," Robert said answering his phone.

"Hi Robert, its JP, put me on speaker phone. I need you and Megan both to hear what I have to say," JP said with a tone of excitement.

Robert put the cell phone on speaker phone so that Megan could be part of the conversation.

"We have not yet cracked the password on the laptop that you found in Seth Brook's room. The Sergeant wants you, Robert, to see if you can, when you get back. She also told me that the address book you found does not have anything important, only Crystal Stone's address. We found nothing in the wallet. But in Seth's suit, that was in the closet, they did find a safe deposit box slip with Sharron Jenkins' name on it. The receipt was made out to Sharron Jenkins for box 25 at the Bank of Denver. I am going over to see what is in it now. I will let you know what I find," JP said before he hung up.

"So have you seen anything suspicious yet?" Robert asked looking at the house.

"No not yet...wait, a limo just pulled up," Megan said.

Robert and Megan watched the car. They saw Crystal exit the house and run over to the limousine. She looked like she was angry at whoever was in the car.

"Call Candice and tell her to follow this car," Megan said to Robert.

"Hi Candy...we need you to follow a black limo with tinted windows, the plate number is 825-ROCCO. Colorado plates..," Robert said.

"Wait...that could be the same limo that dropped her off this morning," Candice said into the phone.

"Maybe we should see who the limo is registered to," Robert said.

"Is she finding out..wait.....the person in the car just handed Crystal a briefcase," Megan said as she watched Crystal talking to someone in the car.

"Who...are you sure...Thank you," Robert said then he hung up.

"You will never guess who the car is registered to?" Robert said writing the name in his notebook.

"Who?" Megan asked wondering who was in the car.

"Valentine's Casino in Black Hawk, Colorado. Now, here is the strange part, the title is owned by Cowboy's Club," Robert said.

"Well, that narrows it down...wait, another car just pulled up. Crystal is getting in," Megan said as she waited for the car to pass and then counting to ten before starting the car to follow. She noticed the car stop at the red light two cars ahead of them. They watched the car turn right at the light when the cars ahead of her went straight. She took a right.

"Robert, I have been going over the case in my mind and I think our mystery woman could be Crystal Stone. She could be our murderer. She knew that Seth Brooks was at the hotel. She could have killed Sharron Jenkins out of jealousy for taking her place as dancing star."

They followed the car to the Cowboy's Club and Crystal got out with Victor Marshall. Just then, Robert's cell phone rang.

"Meg, the limo that Candy was following stopped and picked up Mark Willis and now it's out front. Do you want her to keep tailing it?" Robert asked, as Megan watched Crystal and Victor go through the side door into the club.

"No. We know who the limo belongs to," Megan said trying to think of a way to go undercover to find out what was going on.

Chapter 22

"Okay, what evidence do we have to go on?" Asked Ruth who was standing by the evidence board of the case, examining the clues that they had so far.

"We know that it was a woman covered head to toe like a traditional Muslim that left the envelope for Seth Brooks," Megan said pointing to the photo of the woman dressed as a Muslim.

"I am back," JP said when he came into the room carrying a black briefcase.

"What is in the case?" Ruth asked.

"Let's find out," JP said putting the briefcase on his desk to pick the lock so he could open it. When he finally got the case open they found contracts, photos, and a flash drive. JP took out the flash drive and put it into his computer so that they could view it.

When the file opened, a video appeared on the computer screen. It was Sharron Jenkins.

"Seth, these are the contracts of all the jobs that I have been on since I have been a dancer for the Cowboy's Club. You will find photos of all of the dancers and their names and address, also private phone numbers. I need you to call me about the Cowboy's Club server information in Sophia's office. I am still looking for the investor's client list, but I do know of one. View the video in the other file and you will see who it is. I can't wait for you to get into Denver, call me when you get here and I will give you the other information...I have to go to work now, see you soon," Sharron said and then the video went blank.

Megan picked up the bundle of photos and started to look through them.

JP clicked on the other file on the flash drive. The video showed an empty hotel room, the door opened and in walked Sharron and a woman. They were followed by a man dressed in a business suit.

"I know that man. He works for the government office. His name is Joshua Pratt," Ruth said in a tone of surprise.

"And I know the woman with Sharron. Her name is Janet Chi. Here is her photo with a red X on her face," Megan said holding up the photo of the Asian dancer, and then putting it on the evidence board.

Ruth and the others watched the video. They watched as Sharron and Janet danced for Joshua who sat on the bed. The women took off each other's clothes while Joshua watched. When they were naked, they helped him out of his suit. When he was naked, the girls tied him to the bed and each took their turns on top of him. When they were finished, the girls untied Joshua and let him get dressed. Then, he gave each of them a big bundle of bills. It looked like a couple of grand.

"I will have to call and make another appointment with you girls," Joshua said before he left the room.

"I can't believe that he gave us each three thousand dollars," Sharron said after she counted the money.

"Yeah, that is great for an hour of work. Now give me a thousand to give to the person who set this up. You wait here. I will be back tomorrow," Janet said getting dressed and then leaving.

Sharron locked the door behind Janet and then went to video camera and shut it off.

"Ruth, I think that I need to go undercover as a dancer for the Cowboy's Club. So we can find out what is going on there," Megan said after finishing looking at the photos and putting them into piles.

"No. I don't that is a good idea," Ruth said looking at the pile of photos with red X's and the pile without.

"Meg, why don't you go in as a barmaid instead?" Robert asked.

"I agree with Robert," Ruth said.

"Ruth, the trouble didn't start until Sharron became a dancer. Being a dancer is the only way that I can find out what happened to Sharron Jenkins and Seth Brooks," Megan said pleading her case.

"She has a point, Sarge. Mark Willis, Crystal Stone, and Victor Marshall all know who I am and what I look like," Candice said coming to Megan's defense.

"Ruth, you called Robert and I to help you with this case. So let us help you with it," Megan said.

"Okay, you will need to learn how to strip. Here, there is a sex store on Colfax. Go there and ask for Ellie. I will arrange the rest," Ruth said as she wrote down the directions on a slip of paper for Megan.

Chapter 23

Robert entered the evidence room to see if he could crack the password on Seth Brook's laptop. He knew he has his work cut out for him, but he knew what he had to do. He removed the hard drive out of the laptop.

"JP, I need your computer," Robert said when he got up to the Detective's offices.

"Sure. What do you need it for?" JP asked looking at the hard drive in Robert's hand.

"I need to put this hard drive into your computer."

"Okay, it is all yours."

Robert sat down at JP's computer and went to work.

He took off the cover and placed the hard drive into the universal hard drive port of JP's computer.

"What are you doing?" JP asked.

"I am going to access Seth Brook's laptop. I just hope that I can bypass the password," Robert said.

JP watched Robert click on the start menu of JP's computer, and then go into his user's folder. He found Seth's user file, when he double clicked on the file it was a success.

"I was hoping that this would bypass the password, now let's see what is on this laptop," Robert said.

They looked at the folders. There seemed to be hundreds of them.

"Let's look at this one called passwords," Robert said as he double clicked on the folder.

"It looks like Seth has Gmail, Yahoo. What is the user name and passwords?" JP asked.

"The user name is his first and last name with no caps. The password to all the emails is lower case h-u-g-g-e-r-b-u-g capital S-J," Robert read as JP wrote it down in his notepad.

Robert first went into Seth's Gmail account and found emails from an architect school in Nashville, Tennessee. He found emails about blue prints of buildings, but nothing about Sharron Jenkins.

"Write this architect company down, S&J Architecture & Design in Nashville, Tennessee," Robert said.

"Is there anything about Sharron Jenkins or the Cowboy's Club?" JP asked after he wrote down the information that Robert gave to him.

"No. I am going to check his Yahoo mail now."

Robert opened the first Yahoo email. It was from lovebugS.J. JP pushed his chair over next to Robert so he could also see what was on the computer screen and write the information down.

Robert opened the emails from lovebugS.J so they could read them.

> SETH,
> I AM LETTING YOU KNOW THAT I AM GETTING A PROMOTION AT WORK. I AM GOING TO BE A DANCER, I START NEXT WEEK. MY ROOMMATE GOT ME THE JOB, BUT THERE ARE OTHER GIRLS THAT WORK FOR THE CLUB THAT ARE JEALOUS OF ME. I AM STRONG. I COME FROM TENNESSEE, SO I CAN TAKE IT. I HOPE THAT YOU ARE DOING WELL. I AM SORRY THAT I LEFT THE WAY THAT I DID, BUT IN MY HEART I STILL LOVE YOU AND CARE ABOUT YOU.
> S.J

> SETH,
> I JUST GOT HERE IN DENVER, COLORADO AND LOVING IT. TOMORROW I AM GOING TO LOOK FOR WORK, BUT RIGHT NOW EVERYTHING IS FINE WITH THE MONEY THAT I GOT SINGING AT GILLIAN'S.
> S.J

> SETH,
> I HAVE A JOB, I AM THE NEW BARMAID AT THIS PLACE CALLED THE COWBOY'S CLUB. I AM NOW LIVING WITH ONE OF THE GIRLS. SHE IS THE STAR DANCER. I HAVE TO GO TO WORK NOW. THIS IS MY NEW NUMBER 720-555-5695.
> S.J

Robert checked for more emails from lovebugS.J but found none.

"Check out the next email, the one from DancingStarS.J," JP said.

Robert checked for all the emails from DancingStarS.J and opened the first one.

SETH,

I HAVE FINALLY MADE IT, I AM DANCING THIS WEEK. I AM GOING TO BE DOING A SHOW AT THIS PLACE CALLED VALENTINE'S. IT'S A CASINO IN BLACK HAWK, COLORADO. I GOT YOUR LAST EMAIL SAYING THAT YOU WERE COMING FOR A VISIT. I CAN'T WAIT TO SEE AND TALK TO YOU.

S.J

"Well it is getting late. I am going to call it a day. You should go home. Everyone else has gone for the night. I think even the Sarge went home," JP said yawning.

"Yeah, I think I am going to look at these other emails and find out more about Seth Brooks and his company," Robert said.

"Ok, well the Sergeant will be in around six in the morning," JP said getting up and then leaving to go home.

Robert looked up S&J Architecture & Design in Nashville, Tennessee. He found out that Seth Brooks and Justin Peterson were the owners of the company and their reviews were outstanding. Robert looked at their website and at the blueprints and photos of buildings and homes that they designed. Robert looked at the photos of the employees at the Firm. Justin Peterson had wavy dark brown hair and brown eyes.

'I bet I could pass for this Justin guy.' he thought studying the photo.

Then he read another email from Sharron to Seth.

SETH,

I HAVE TO TELL YOU THAT MY FRIEND JANET HAS GONE MISSING. SHE WAS THE ONE OF THE DANCERS, AND ALSO ONE OF MY ROOMMATES. WHEN WE WENT TO BLACK HAWK AND DID A PRIVATE SHOW, SHE LEFT OUR HOTEL ROOM AND NEVER CAME BACK. I HAVE SENT YOU A SAFETY DEPOSIT SLIP IN THE MAIL. I HAVE TO GO. THIS IS THE LAST EMAIL I CAN SEND UNDER THIS ID.

S.J

Robert looked at the clock; it was two in the morning. It was too late for him to drive to his farm so he decided that he would sleep on the sofa in the officer's lounge.

Chapter 24

Inside the Mirror

Robert brought Crystal to his ranch, where she could rest and he could go out and get food for her. After he brought her to the main house, he had to find her something to feed on.

"Crystal, you stay here. I will back soon," Robert said and then left the ranch.

Robert drove up and down Colfax until he found what he was looking for. He saw an Asian woman. She had dark brown hair cut into a bob style. She was standing by the street sign. He watched as she went up to cars that pulled up to the corner. She was wearing a short black mini skirt, black stilettos, and a white blouse with red roses.

"So you are looking for some action, are you my little morsel?" Robert said to himself pulling up to the corner and stopping beside her.

"Are you looking for some action?" Robert asked her as he leaned over to the passenger's window of the car and called to the woman. She walked over to his car and leaned in the window.

"Hi my name is Lilly. You looking for a good time?" She asked licking her full, glossy, red lips looking in at Robert.

"So, what do you charge for your time Lilly?" Robert asked and then smiled slyly like a fox.

"Well first show me your package before we talk business, so I know you are not a cop," Lilly said looking in at Robert as he unzipped his dark blue slacks and showed himself to her.

"Ok, let me ask you, do you want to make it really interesting? I have a couple of friends...are you bi-sexual?" Lilly asked winking.

Robert nodded his head yes, lying to her.

"Janet and Abe, come over here, there is someone I want you to meet," Lilly called to a couple about three feet from her.

Robert saw a young Asian woman. She was wearing a short black skirt, a short black leather jacket, and five inch heels. Her long dark straight hair was blowing in the wind as she walked. A well built man with long black hair followed behind her. He had on a white silk shirt under his black leather jacket and tight fitting jeans with holes .The man was also Asian. Lilly and her friends got into Robert's car, Lilly in the front seat with him, and her friends in the back seat.

"How much?" Robert asked.

"How about a thousand each," Lilly asked.

"Sure, that would be ok," Robert said and then took the money out of his wallet and gave it to Lilly.

"This is Janet and Abe," Lilly said introducing her friends handing each of them their cut.

"So where are we going?" Lilly asked as she began to undo Robert's pants. She put her hand inside and fondled him.

"We are going to my place, I have a farm not too far from here," Robert said as he drove.

When Robert and his guests got to the farm, they came to a big wooden sign that read Tower Estates. It hung over a gate. The farm was encircled by a twelve foot red brick wall so no one from the street could see the farm. He pushed the remote that he had on his visor and the gate opened and closed after he drove through. They drove up a deserted private road for three miles. The road had nothing but trees on both sides. They then came to a long dirt road that took them to Robert's ranch. Robert pulled the car up to one of the buildings and stopped.

Robert got out of the car and so did his guests. The farm came alive with the sounds of animals. Robert escorted his guests to the porch of the building. He opened the front door which led to a large living room.

"Would you like something to drink?" Robert asked as he went to the bar that separated the kitchen from the living room.

"Do you have a bottle of wine that we all can share?" Lilly asked while the trio made themselves comfortable on the large black leather sofa.

"Yes, I do. Would you all like a glass?" Robert asked.

"Yes. Do you mind if we smoke?" Janet asked.

"No, I don't mind. You will find an ashtray on the coffee table," Robert said as he brought out the wine bottle and placed it on the coffee table. He handed each of his guests a crystal wine glass, and then turned on some music.

"So what's your name?" Abe asked taking a sip of his wine.

Robert thought of giving a fake name, but it wouldn't matter what name he gave them.

"Robert. So what do you three do? Dance or what?"

"Yes, we do. Would you like us to dance for you?" Lilly asked as she looked up at Robert. Robert was standing beside the coffee table looking down her shirt at her cleavage.

"Why don't you sit down and get comfortable honey," Janet said as she got up from the sofa and walked up to him. She took his big hand into her tiny delicate soft hand. Then she led him to the sofa between Lilly and Abe so he could sit between them. They both rubbed his thighs as Lilly leaned over and kissed Abe, who inched his hand up to Robert's crotch. Just then Sharron Jenkins sultry voice came over the speakers with 'Take Me'. Janet started to dance in the middle of the living room. She swayed her body erotically as she danced. Abe got up and started dancing with her and rubbing his hands all over her body while kissing her. Robert watched and then Lilly got up and started to dance also. Janet sat back down next to Robert as they watched Lilly and Abe dance for them. As Abe and Lilly danced, he slowly and seductively unbuttoned her blouse. Robert watched as Abe removed Lilly's blouse and exposed her white lace bra. Abe kissed her neck and then her soft lips. Robert was really enjoying the show, as Janet was rubbing her hand over the front of his pants feeling him get hard. Janet started to strip also without knowing what Robert had on his mind. She took off her clothes until she only had on her see through thong.

The song ended and another erotic song started to play.

Abe moved the coffee table into the middle of the room, so that he could sit on it to give Robert a real show. He slowly undressed until he was just wearing his white silk shirt. Then he sat on the edge of the oak coffee table as Lilly got on her hands and knees and crawled up to him. She pushed his legs apart and rubbed herself on him. She took off her lace bra to reveal her perky breasts.

Robert looked at Janet and kissed her. He grabbed her hair and pulled her head back exposing her slender neck. He began to lick her soft, tender flesh. He thought she smelled of vanilla and roses mixed with sensuality. She tried to pull away from the hold that he had on her, but he only held her tighter. Lilly was now straddling Abe, who was holding her by the waist as she let him enter her.

Robert was getting more excited. He threw Janet on to the sofa. She gasped in surprise at how lustful and forceful he became. He ripped her thong off with one hand and with the other he undid his pants, and then he entered her. When she felt him inside her, she enjoyed him, so she let him take her body as she did his. Robert snuggled his mouth into the soft part of her neck, and at the same time he spilled his seed, as he sank his fangs into her flesh. He tasted the sweetness of her blood as the crimson fluid ran down her neck. That's when the moans got the attention of the dancers as they watched the lovers on the sofa. Janet moaned as Robert pushed his hard body against her and suckled on her now bloody neck.

Lilly screamed when she saw her friend's blood run down her neck onto her pert nipple of her breast. Janet tried to push away, now screaming. Lilly and Abe ran to help their friend but as they tried to pull Robert away from his Asian meal, he bit Janet's neck again to get more of her crimson life. Robert could feel her life slip away as he felt her heart pounding inside of his head. The pounding sounded like the drum beat in a dance club. The pounding was so loud that it was giving him a headache, then the drumming came to a rise and it faded away. That is when he knew he had to stop feeding before the pumping of her heart stopped. With a feeling of regret he stopped sucking and let go of Janet's limp body. Lilly and Abe ran out of the house screaming, when they realized that he had killed their friend. Robert watched as Janet's body convulsed. She gasped for air, and then her life slipped away.

"Crystal my love, it is time to feed," Robert whispered into her ear to wake the hunger.

She opened her eyes and looked up at him.

"Robert, I am weak and hungry," she said as tears came to her eyes.

"I know my darling. It's time. Can you walk?" he asked as he helped the frail vampiress to her feet and out onto the balcony. He grabbed a hold of her and jumped to the ground. Robert knew that his victims would be hiding somewhere, because they didn't have time to reach the road yet. Even if they did reach the road, they couldn't open the gate or go over the twelve foot wall. Robert sniffed the air, he could smell them. Lilly was in the field between the main house and the barn. He picked up Crystal and glided over to the barn and hid. They waited for Lilly to come to them.

"Abe where are you?" Lilly whispered.

"I am over here," Abe's voice answered from the other side of the barn.

"Here comes something to feed on now honey," Robert whispered in Crystal's ear. He could hear the clicking of Lilly's heels on the stone walkway between the house and barn.

"Abe, where the fuck are you?" Lilly called softly.

"I am over here by the house and the barn," Abe called back softly.

Robert and Crystal waited in the darkness of the two buildings ready to pounce.

Lilly walked closer and closer, Robert could smell the sweet fear she gave off as she came into the darkness. He knew that this sweet Lilly morsel was unknowingly walking right into his grasp. When she got close, he grabbed her and held her in front of him, with his hand over her mouth to stifle her screams. Poor Lilly kicked and punched at his arms, trying to break free. That was when Robert bared his fangs. He looked at Crystal who also bared her sharp fangs, impatiently waiting to be fed. He bit down on Lilly's slender neck and started the blood flowing for Crystal to drink. Crystal fed like a nursing cub. Robert pulled her away from her feeding so she would not take too much and get sick. She looked at him with a wild look and crawled back into the shadows of the house and the barn.

Robert drank more, then he motioned for Crystal that it was time for her to feed some more. She took Lilly's body in her arms and bit down on the front of her throat and started the flow of blood. The blood flowed like water from a faucet, but it was too much for her to drink. She spat the blood as it gushed from of Lilly's open throat. Finally, Robert pushed her away from Lilly's now dead body.

"You can't feed on her anymore. She's dead. You can't feed on the dead," he explained to her as he helped her to her feet and away from the dead body. The vampiress wiped the blood off of her face with the back of her hand. The Cinderella gown was now stained crimson red. Crystal looked at Lilly's body and then back at Robert and whispered.

"I want more. Please Robert! I want more."

He could not deny her food now.

Abe walked into the light shining from the porch. Crystal and Robert were still hidden in the shadows, watching.

"Lilly, where the fuck are you?" Abe called quietly.

"Crystal can you smell him?" Robert whispered.

"Yes I can. He smells sweet and musty," Crystal whispered back.

"Be careful not to spook him. When he comes close, I want you to ever so slowly grab him and show yourself to him. When you do this, seduce him with your eyes. When you have him under your spell that is when you attack. Bite him just like I did Lilly. Do you understand Crystal? You will only have one chance."

Crystal watched as Abe came closer. When he was within her reach, she grabbed his arm. He turned to see who was grabbing him. At the sight of her face he fell in love. He was captured by her beauty, her full luscious ruby lips, and her pale white skin. Her long blonde hair was blowing in the wind, but her eyes are what entrapped him the most. She knew that she had him. She licked her lips, and then she pulled him into the darkness. She bit down on his strong neck and sucked until she tasted his blood. She was in ecstasy as she licked and bit the man. His white silk tee-shirt was now a deep red as the blood from his neck stained the silk. Abe could not stop her as she ripped at his clothes and cried out as she took his life fluid into her. He fell to the ground and let Crystal take him. When she had enough she savagely ripped out Abe's throat and licked the blood off her lips, and then wiped her mouth with his shirt.

Robert took Abe's body and put it into the wheelbarrow that was next to the barn. He threw Lilly's body on top. He needed to show Crystal how to get rid of the bodies of her victims that she didn't turn. He left the vampiress and the bodies. He went into the kitchen and got a big black trash bag. Then went into the living room where he looked down at Janet's body and scooped it up into the bag. He noticed a spot of blood that had pooled on the floor where her body was. He wiped it up with the dead woman's blouse, and then he threw her clothes into the bag and tied it closed. He threw the trash bag on top of the other two bodies when he got back to Crystal. She watched him as he wheeled the cart over to the pigpen, and one by one he threw the bodies into the pig slop.

"Here piggys! Time for your evening treats," Robert called to the hog and piglets in the pen. He and Crystal watched as the hogs and piglets devoured their three guests, leaving nothing behind, not even bones.

Mirror

Robert awoke and shook his head and wiped the sweat from his forehead with his hand. He opened his eyes and found himself on the sofa in the officer's lounge.

Chapter 25

"Were you here all night?" JP asked, walking over to his desk.

"Yeah, I slept on the sofa in the officer's lounge," Robert said looking up at JP.

"So, that's Seth Brooks' emails?"

"Yes. I found some more emails on aol.com, I am going through all of them."

"What else did you find in the emails? Does any of them explain what Sharron was talking about when she mentioned the Cowboy's Club server?" JP asked.

"Here is an email from another email address, CountryGirl@aol.com," Robert said as he pulled up the email to show JP what it said.

> COUNTRYBOY,
> THE CC FILES, AND CLIENT INFORMATION IS ON THE SERVER. THE ONE NAMED THE COWBOYSCLUBMW WHICH IS IN THE FIRST OFFICE. THE ID IS COWGIRLS AND THE PASSWORD IS 12@#MYGIRLSMW. THE EMAILS ARE ALL THERE. ALSO, THE PASSWORDS TO ALL OF THE EMAIL ADDRESSES IS COWBOYSCLUB#1STARDANCERS.
> COUNTRYGIRL

JP wrote the information on his notepad.

"This is the response that Seth gave to her."

> COUNTRYGIRL
> DID YOU GET ME THE JOB REMODELING THE CLUB YET?
> COUNTRYBOY

> COUNTRYBOY
> THE PLAN IS IN MOTION. YOU ARE TO WAIT FOR THE CALL.
> REMEMBER, STAY AT THE SHERATON. I WILL FIND YOU.

COUNTRYGIRL

"Good morning Gentlemen," Ruth said, as she entered the office.

"Good morning Ruth. I got into Seth Brooks' hard drive. We found some things that you should have a look at," Robert said.

"What did you find? JP, take the photos of the dancers and put them into the police computer. Find out if they have records or warrants and let me know," Ruth said sitting in JP's chair after he got up.

Chapter 26

Megan walked into the sex store and saw the XXX rated videos next to the checkout counter. She watched a tall thin man stocking some lube on the shelf in back of the counter. The man looked back at the counter and saw Megan standing there watching him.

"Oh Sweetie, what can I help you with?" The man said in soft feminine voice. She looked at the man. He had spiked pink hair, a gold small hoop earring stuck out of his bottom lip. She thought he looked like a kid from a gothic dance club.

"I am here to see with Ellie. My name is Megan," She said and then smiled.

"She is in the back. I'll get her for you," the store clerk said as he left her at the counter and walked to the back of the store. She could see that the clerk was wearing a leather thong over his tight orange jeans. She watched until he disappeared into the back room.

When he returned a woman was with him. Megan noticed the woman had long, black, straight hair. She was about five feet and six inches tall. She looked very fit and her skin was a cocoa brown color. She was wearing a tight, short black leather dress.

"Hello, you must be Megan Sapphire. Aunt Ruth told me that you needed me to show you how to dance and strip," Ellie said as she greeted Megan with a hand shake.

"Yes. I've never stripped, but need to learn. I am a fast learner though," Megan said and then smiled.

"Well let's start then. I have a lot to teach you. Come with me," Ellie said.

Megan followed Ellie to the back of the store.

"I am a dance instructor for men and woman that want to learn how to dance. I have been a teacher for about two years now. Aunt Ruth thought that it would be in my best interest to be a teacher not a stripper. That is why she got me this store and this dance studio. So how do you know Aunt Ruth? Do you work for her at the police department?"

"No, I used to, but now I work for myself. I left the department about a year ago, but Ruth and I stay in touch."

"Why did you leave the department? Was it because my Aunt is a bitch sometimes? You can tell me. I know how she can be. When I lived with her she was."

"No, it had nothing to do with Ruth. It was for personal advancement in my career."

"Okay, then. Here is the dance studio," Ellie said as she unlocked the door to the studio. Megan and Ellie walked inside. She turned on the lights and put on some music. Megan waited for Ellie to return from the music booth.

"Now let's begin. To be a stripper you have to dance like you are making love," Ellie said when she came back to the dance area.

"I don't really know all that much about dancing," Megan said shyly.

"Well just sit down and watch me. I will show you some easy moves," Ellie said as the music came over the loud speaker. The music was very sultry. She swayed to the music erotically as she moved her hips to the music.

"Okay Megan, you show me what I just showed you?"

Megan got up and started to sway to the music. Ellie placed her hands on Megan's hips to show her how to move erotically.

"You are doing great. Now I want you to think of dancing for someone that makes you hot. Think of how you would have sex with them," Ellie said as she watched as Megan moved her body in rhythm to the music.

"Okay, I want you to practice that tonight. Try thinking about your lover and how you would make love to them. Your next lesson is going to be tomorrow morning? How does six sound?"

"I guess that will be ok. How many lessons do you think, I will need before I can pass as a stripper?"

"I would say at least three to get down a routine that would get you a job. After, you will have to come in three times a week if you want to get noticed at the club. Then, I would say, four times a week for more lessons to learn other routines. Megan, dancing in a club is hard work. You will have to know how to lap dance and pole dance. I am teaching a pole dancing class this week I think you should join us for that."

"I will, and thank you, Ellie, for teaching me all that I need to learn."

"Here is a tip for you, this is what I used to do when I was a dancer. Practice your dancing and stripping at home in private and always in front of a full length mirror. This will show you how you are doing, and show you what you still need to work on. Keep this in mind Megan, always, if your dancing doesn't turn you on, it won't turn on the customers either," Ellie said.

Chapter 27

Megan walked to the door of Ellie's porn shop and found the door locked. She could see Ellie at the counter doing paper work. She knocked on the glass door and Ellie looked up and saw her at the door.

"Well good morning Megan how are you? Are you ready to do some dancing?" Ellie asked after she opened the door and let her into the store.

"I think I am awake. I made it here, so that counts for something," Megan said and then laughed.

"Well there is coffee in the back. Why don't we go in and have some. I want to talk to you about what we are going to be working on today. I think I am going to have Andy work with you this morning. He knows the club music and what is "in" for the club dances. That is what you will be learning this morning, also some romantic dances and how to take tips," Ellie said.

"When do we begin?"

"Andy will be here soon," Ellie said as she poured herself a cup of coffee and then another for Megan.

"Hey girls. Coffee, yes, I think I'll join you. I had a night for the history books. Let me tell you. I went out to the Church, you know that Goth club that I took you to last week El. Well, any who, I met up with some friends and the club was full, so we went to another club. It was that new club, Orange on Broadway. I don't think it is going to last, we only went there because a friend was the DJ. By the time I got home and crashed the sun was coming up. I would kill for some speed or cocaine right about now. Just fucking with ya, El. So what is on the agenda for yours truly today?" Andy said pouring himself a cup of coffee.

"Megan this is Andy. You are going to help Megan with her dancing. Here's a list of things that she needs to learn," Ellie said introducing the two and then handing Andy a list.

"Hey girl, nice to know you. It looks like I am going to help you with your dancing. I hope you are ready to learn from the 'Dancing Bitch'," Andy said and then smiled coyly as he pointed to the words on his coffee cup.

"Okay, I am going to leave you two now so I can do some work. Andy did the shipment of dildos come in last night?" Ellie asked.

"Yes. Andrea put them in the store room. Who is working this morning, while I'm showing Megan how to dance?" Andy asked.

"You are looking at who is working this morning. I'm also thinking of calling Andrea to see if she would like some overtime," Ellie said leaving the room.

"So what do you do for work? Are you a stripper and need some dance lessons? Or are you learning to strip and dance for your man?" Andy asked trying to figure out why Megan wanted to learn how to dance.

"I am going to be working for the Cowboy's Club," Megan said not really lying, but not actually telling the truth either.

"Wow! So you are starting straight at the top. Be careful, I knew a girl that worked for them. Her name was Janet, she said that the owner and dancers can be real assholes. But so was Janet's boyfriend, though, I believe that is why she left town. Well, what do you say we get to work? I have a lot to show you," Andy said getting up from the table with his cup. Megan followed him into the dance studio. Andy put on some dance music with a beat.

"The rules to dancing are simple. Rule number one, feel the music. Close your eyes," Andy said.

Megan did as she was told and closed her eyes. She was surprised that she could feel the beats of the music. She began to sway her hips to the beat.

"Okay, that is great, you can feel the music... now what is the music telling you? What do you feel? What is the music making you think about? When you know and feel what the music is telling you, that is when you can feel the emotion of the music. Let the music capture your heart, body, and soul. Now allow your body and the music take control of you and dance the way you are feeling."

Megan started to sway and move her hips back and forth. She felt her heart pound to the rhythm of the music.

"Now let's try another type of music. A more aggressive kind where it makes you feel like a dominating bitch. I want you to do the same thing, close your eyes and let the music take you," Andy said changing the music.

Megan did what she was told and she moved to the music. As she touched her body with her hands she felt herself go to a dark place, a place that she didn't understand. She opened her eyes and stopped dancing. She felt like she was in a dream like the one she had before finding out Seth Brooks was dead. She opened her eyes and stopped dancing.

"I think I need to take a break," Megan said startled by where the music took her.

"I understand, the music took you to an uncomfortable place that you believe is not a good place for you, but it is a good place. It's just that you are not used to it. Before taking a break, let's dance to some club music," Andy said.

Megan watched as Andy showed her the moves and then she did them with him.

"Now let's have some fun dance with me, show me your moves," Andy said as he took her hand and danced with her, then the music turned into a slow dance.

"You are going to have to know the basics of all of the sexy, emotional dances. Such as the waltz, the tango, dirty dancing, salsa, and yes even ballet. You are going to need them with pole dancing. I was a ballroom dancer in New York before I moved here. Okay, why don't you take a break. I am going to show you something that you have to be aware of when you are dancing on stage," Andy said as he escorted Megan to the chair in the back of the room. Andy took a dollar out of his wallet and gave it to Megan. He then started dancing around in the middle of the floor like he was a stripper.

"When you're dancing on stage you have to be alert, look the people holding money out for you. Hold out the dollar to me, watch me. Notice how I am swaying over to get the dollar. Don't just get the money, dance in front of them for a moment like you want to fuck them. That is their fantasy, they want to fuck you. Keep eye contact with them, because if you are not making them horny then they will not stay. Your job is to make them horny so they will stay, so you have to dance like a hot slut," Andy said and then he crawled over to her like a cat, and took the dollar into his teeth. He then stood up and grinded his pelvis in front of her face.

"And, Megan, most of all remember to enjoy yourself," Ellie said coming into the room to see how the dance lesson was going.

"That's right, always enjoy yourself. Why don't we show Ellie what we learned so far," Andy said.

Ellie watched as Megan danced and showed her all the dance moves that she learned.

"Megan, why don't we go for lunch before the next lesson? I am going to be your teacher for the next lesson," Ellie said.

"Okay, that sounds great," Megan said.

"Andy you take your break, then go relieve Andrea so she can take hers," Ellie said before she and Megan left the store.

"Okay, this lesson is going to be about what to wear, and what character you want to play. When you do a character you don't just act like the character. You have to take on the persona of that character, just like when you do when go undercover on a case. The music you pick has to go with that character also. Don't rush, take your time, don't start stripping when you first get on stage. Let the music take you into another zone give the audience a show before you take anything off," Ellie said as she danced around to the sound of the erotic music that was playing. When the drums started to play she moved her hips in a sensual circle with the beat. Megan watched Ellie move and then she tried to mimic what she was doing.

"When you feel like you have captured your audience, it's time to slowly unbutton your blouse. If you are wearing a dress, unzip the zipper, but do it slowly and erotically," Ellie said as she slowly unbuttoned the top button of her white silk blouse. Megan followed and unbuttoned the first button of her white dress shirt.

"Now, slowly move your hands as if your hands were your lovers. Unbutton the rest of the buttons, remember to keep dancing and moving your body while you do it," Ellie said as she watched Megan follow her directions.

"That's good. Now when all the buttons are undone, let the fabric open showing your bra," Ellie said watching as Megan let the shirt open exposing her black lace bra and her cleavage.

"If you were wearing a loose blouse you would let it fall off your body to the floor, like this," Ellie said as she unbuttoned her blouse and letting the silk fabric fall off her shoulders, as the blouse fell down her arms it created a pool of white silk at her feet.

"Take off your shirt the sexiest way that you can," Ellie said.

Megan slowly took off her shirt and let it fall from her fingers onto the floor beside her.

"That was great. Now unzip your skirt, slowly pull the zipper down. Then slowly pull your skirt down giving a little tease. Slowly pull it down with your fingertips then pull it back up," Ellie said as she showed Megan how she wanted her to do it. Megan followed suit and did the same thing Ellie did.

"Wow, that will turn the audience on. Do it again, but this time let your skirt fall off your body onto the floor and dance out of it," Ellie said and then showed Megan how to it.

"Be sure that you step out of your skirt, then away from it so you won't trip. I want you to touch yourself, when it is close to the end of the song you are going to take off your bra. If you can't reach it, ask someone in the audience to help you with the clasp. If you do that you will get kudos with the audience and also the manager of the club. Dance over to me and kneel in front of me with your back to me, ask me to help you," Ellie said as she sat in the chair next to where Megan was dancing.

"Will you help me?" Megan asked in a sexy tone and then smiled.

"That is great, any questions?"

"What happens if the music stops before I am done?" Megan asked.

"That is a great question, and I have a great answer. You never allow that to happen. That is why you have to practice your dance at least three times every day so you know how much time it will take you," Ellie said.

"Why don't you come back at ten tonight? I have a late night class for pole dancing. Wear something loose and sexy, we will also discuss what you are planning to wear to your audition," Ellie said.

Megan started to leave the room, but Ellie stopped her from leaving.

"Where are you going? You have your ballet lesson. Andy will be right in."

"What do you mean?"

"Put on those shorts and tank top. After you're dressed, go and relax in the break room, get a snack and a bottle of water. You wanted to be a dancer? This is what it takes to be one, weeks and months and sometimes even years of lessons and practices. But we only have three days to get you ready, so we have work fast," Ellie explained before she left the room so that Megan could dress.

Chapter 28
Inside the Mirror

Megan ran after Seth's slave and caught her in the round room. The woman was screaming. Megan dragged the woman by the arm back into the room that she ran from.

"Listen, I am not going to hurt you. I need you to forget what happened here," Megan said and then put her hand over the woman's eyes.

"You will forget me. You will forget my face. You will forget this room. You will forget what happened. When you feel the cool air of the night, your memory will be erased of everything you've been through tonight," Megan chanted and then removed her hand and the woman was asleep. She left the woman sleeping on the stone bench.

Megan now knew what power was in the stiletto ritual dagger. Now was the time to go somewhere private were she could meet with Robert. She knew just the place, the old ghost town in Central City.

Mirror

Megan awoke to the sound of her alarm going off. She didn't want to get up, it felt like she just went to bed, and her body was sore. She had trouble getting out of bed, but she had to. She had one more lesson and this one was a practice lesson. She got up and took a shower. It felt good, letting the hot water of the shower caress and drip over her tight and sore joints and muscles. She thought about what she was going to wear for the audition. She decided on a leather dress and five inch black heels, and maybe her leather jacket. She got out of the shower and plugged in her curlers so they could heat up while she put on her make-up.

When Megan got to Ellie's porn store, she was standing at the door waiting for her.

"Wow, you look great. Is this what you are going to wear to do your dance for your audition at the club?" Ellie asked as she walked around Megan checking out the outfit.

"I thought it would be a good outfit, because I will be able to slowly unzip the front. Then let it fall open and then fall to the floor easily. It's also sleeveless," Megan said and then took off the jacket to show her.

"Great thinking, now you are thinking like a stripper. What do you have on underneath? I see you have no stockings or nylons,"

"No. I thought it would be ok not to wear any. I am however wearing black lace panties and a matching bra."

"Let me give you something...let's say a present for being such a great student," Ellie said and then went over to the garter belts. She picked out a red lace suspender garter belt and sheer thigh highs. She then picked out some red lace panties and lace push up bra to match. The last item was black thigh high boots with a black seam in the back.

"Here put these on and let's see how they look," Ellie said as she handed Megan the items that she picked out for her.

"I will be in the studio. Come in when you are done."

Megan entered the dance studio. She noticed Ellie and Andy sitting in the chairs next to the stripper pole waiting.

"Megan, show us what you learned," Ellie said.

Megan went into her dance. She picked music that was sexy, with an erotic beat. She moved her hips to the beat of the drums. She swayed to the sultry music. She danced over to her audience as she opened up her legs and then bent down and touched her calf. Megan moved her hands up her legs very slowly. She then moved the zipper down just a bit for a little tease. She danced to the stripper pole and wrapped her leg around the pole. She unzipped her dress as she leaned her body back until her long raven hair touched the floor.

"Great job! I think you are ready to audition," Ellie said as she and Andy clapped when Megan was done with the dance.

Chapter 29

After Crystal finished her dance, Mark went over to the dance floor and picked up her clothes and then followed her into the dressing room.

"Crystal, I need you to do me a favor," Mark said when they reached the dressing room door.

"Who is it and what do I have to do? I thought I was done with that when I became the star again," Crystal said as she looked down at the floor with a shameful look on her face.

"Crystal darling, you're not the real star. Your turn was last month. I only let you stay the star, because of what happened to Sharron. Besides, you are great at what you...ha, ha...let's just say you are great with doing the favors that I ask of you. This time I need you to do a car show. There is a client that will want to spend time with you. I told him that you would give him the platinum package. You make sure he has a good time and do anything that he wants," Mark said as he put his arms around Crystal and then he kissed her on the lips. She just smiled when the kiss ended and nodded her head. She went into the dressing room and closed the door behind her. She held her clothes and looked at herself in the mirror that hung over the make-up table. She laughed and then she cried as her mascara tears rolled down her checks.

She felt like she had died inside.

"Crystal, I need you to do a private dance for a bachelor party, they have paid for a completely nude dance," Mark said through the closed door before opening it. Crystal looked at her employer in the mirror when he came into the dressing room.

"Crystal, don't cry. You knew that you would have to do this after your turn at being the star dancer. You're still Crystal Star, everyone's sexual fantasy," Mark said looking at Crystal's tear stained face.

"What do they want?" Crystal asked as she felt vulnerable for crying in front of Mark. She wiped the tears away then stood up and faced him with her head held up high.

Crystal heard the music began to play a sultry slow tango song. She grabbed the stripper's pole and the curtain opened. As the music played, she danced. She was dressed in a long red cape, and red spiked heeled thigh high boots. She swayed as the female voice started to come through the music.

"There was a young woman who was walking through the woods to see her grandmother.

She stopped when she was approached by a big bad wolf of a man."

The woman's voice said in the song. Crystal danced for the men that sat around the stage. As she danced they threw money at her feet. She erotically pulled off her red velvet gloves with her teeth, and moved her body in a sexy sway. Her eyes were getting glossy as they filled with tears. She moved to the edge of the stage. She laid on the stage and spread her legs to show her red thong to the men trying to reach for her. After she closed her legs and got on her hands and knees and crawled to the middle of the stage to the stripper pole. She climbed the pole until she could put her feet into the strap at the top. She then let go of the pole and let her body fall back until she was hanging upside down. The cape fell open exposing her red lace bra and thong. Crystal slowly unfastened her bra and let it fall to the stage below, exposing her full breasts. She then pushed the button on the pole below her. The pole began to slowly turn. She ripped at her thong until the red lace fabric gave way, showing the men her very sacred place and made her feel vulnerable. When her thong fell to the floor she was spinning around in circles. She undid the clasp of the cape at her throat and let it fall into a red velvet pool below her. She was naked except for her boots. All of the men in the room gasped at her beauty. Crystal unhooked her foot from the strap and slid down the pole like she was a firewoman. She danced around the pole, then got on her hands and knees and crawled to the edge of the stage. She laid on the stage and opened her legs exposing herself to the men.

"What a fucking show! That was the great Crystal Star," Mark said over the microphone at the DJ booth in back of the stage.

Crystal stood on the stage as tears rolled down her face knowing what was going to happen next.

"Now we are going to start amateur night, then we will announce our winner. But first, we will draw the winner for an half an hour in our heaven room with Crystal Stone our star dancer," Mark said as he made his way to the stage and stood beside Crystal, who was holding a glass fish bowl that held the names of the men in the room. Mark took out a folded slip of paper out of the bowl and unfolded it.

"Our winner is Johnny Cox."

"So Megan it looks like you are ready for your audition. How are you going to start a relationship between you and Mr. Willis?" Ruth asked as Megan made herself comfortable in the chair she was sitting in.

"I was thinking of playing the same role as Sharron. I just moved here from Nashville. I am staying with a friend but I have to find somewhere else to live."

"I will set up your cover for you. Megan I want you to be careful. Mark Willis could be our killer."

Megan walked into the Cowboy's Club. She was greeted by the smell of cigarette and cigar smoke. She was making her way to the bar when someone grabbed her by the arm. She looked at the owner of the hand, it was Victor Marshall.

"It is amateur night for ladies. Are you here to dance?" Victor asked, looking her up and down.

"Yes I am, also I would like to speak with the owner of the club for a job," Megan said in a sultry tone to her voice.

"If you dance for us tonight, and if you are any good, I'll see what I can do to help you."

"Are you the owner?"

"No. I am just about everything but the owner. Come on, I will show you to the back."

Megan followed Victor to the back of the stage. They walked to the middle of the room. A blonde woman was dancing on stage. She was dressed as a teacher. She was standing next to a chalkboard. Megan watched the woman dance and take off her glasses and then she took the pins out her hair. Her blonde hair fell as she bent over.

"This way to the dressing rooms, you will be dancing next," Victor said as he escorted Megan through the opened side of the black velvet curtain.

"So what music do you want?"

"I don't know. What music do you think I should use?" Megan asked sounding like she didn't know what she was doing.

"I will get you something sexy and hot. You just dance to it and take off your clothes, and make the audience cum in their pants, just like you are about to make me do. What is your name?"

"Nina Keller, but you can call me Nina," Megan said as she took the clip out of her hair and let it fall like raven black curtains down her back and shoulders.

"Wow. I think I am going to call you Raven instead. You look like a raven with that curly black hair and those blue eyes," Victor said as he watched Megan get herself ready to go out on stage. He regretfully left her to go and announcer her to the stage.

"That was great, Amy. I wish all the teachers were as hot and sexy as you when I was in school. Let's keep our amateur night going with another hot bitch. When you see her long curly black hair you will understand why we call our next contestant Raven!" Victor's voice came over the speakers and then Megan could hear the sultry sound of the music.

Megan danced her way on to the stage. She swayed her body in front of the men that sat by the stage holding out dollar bills for her. She started the dance very slowly. Her hands held over the top of her cleavage. She danced around the stage and slowly and seductively unzipped her tight leather dress. She turned around so the audience could see her red lace bra, the crowd cheered and begged for more. She danced over to the edge of the stage, and then got down on her hands and knees and crawled over to a young man sitting with a man that looked like his father.

"It is my son's twenty-first birthday, would you dance for him?" The older man asked pointing at the younger man sitting next to him.

Megan went to the edge of stage in front of the birthday boy. She then took the young man's hand in hers and put his hand up to her zipper. He unzipped the dress the rest of the way down as her dress flew open, showing them what she had underneath. She erotically danced in front of the young man, and seduced him with her body. She slipped out of her dress and let it fall to the floor. Now she was just in her bra, matching panties and garter belt. She got down really close to the young man's face and pushed her cleavage into his face. His father slipped him a hundred dollar bill and he put the bill into Megan's cleavage. She undid her bra showing the audience her breasts and pert round nipples. The audience applauded and yelled for more, then the stage curtain went down and Victor came on the stage.

"Let's hear it for our Raven," he said and then went in back of the curtain.

"How do you think I did?" Megan asked as Victor gave her a silk robe to put on.

"That was fucking great."

"So do you think that I will get a job?"

"There is someone that you asked to meet, follow me," Victor said as they made their way to the bar.

Mark Willis was standing beside a barmaid who held a tray of empty glasses.

"You best get back to work. We will discuss this later," Mark said to the woman sternly as he slapped her on the ass.

"Mark, this is our Raven, she would like to ask you for a job," Victor said when he and Megan got to where Mark Willis was standing beside the bar.

"Well my dear that was one hell of a dance. I love the way that you allowed that young man to help you with your zipper," Mark said as he took Megan's hand and kissed it.

"Mr. Willis, could I pay this young lady for a private dance for my son? It's his twenty-first birthday," the man from the audience asked.

"I am sorry sir, but this young lady is not on the payroll yet," Mark said to the man.

"Vic, go find Crystal and tell her to give these two gentlemen a dance. Tell her to give them the premium dance," Mark said to Victor who was standing beside Megan.

"Yes. Gentlemen if you will come with me," Victor said as he escorted the men away to find Crystal.

"Well it looks like you have a job if you want it," Mark said to Megan.

"Yes, I would. I just moved here from Nashville. I am staying with a friend right now, but I need to get another place to live soon."

"Well, you call me and we can get together and do the paper work. Then I will have you meet with Sophia, when she gets back, to sign the contracts," Mark said as he gave Megan his business card.

"Thank you Mr. Willis."

"No problem. Call me Mark. I would like you start next week."

"I may have to move next week."

"I will tell you what, if you start next week. I will find you a place to live. I believe one of our dancers is looking for a roommate."

"Thank you Mark, I will be ready to start next week."

Chapter 30

"Megan did you get the job at the Cowboy's Club?" Ruth asked.

"Yes I did. I start next week. I am going to stay with one of the dancers. I hope that it is Crystal Stone. I will know soon. Mark is going to tell me when he calls."

"Where did you tell him you were staying?"

"I told him that I am staying with a friend, but I have to move next week. I have to meet with a woman named Sophia and sign some paperwork. How is the cover profile going for me?"

"I'm having Candice work on your cover."

"Okay, I told Victor that my name is Nina Keller."

"Ruth, there is a call for you. On line one. Megan I am glad you are here, I need you to come with me and take your photo for your cover," Candy said when she came into the office.

After Megan and Candy left, Ruth answered the phone.

"Hello...Yes this is she...Okay I will send someone...no we will contact her and let her know...Okay thank you for checking that for me...Anything we can do for you let us know...Okay bye," Ruth said and then hung up.

JP and Robert came into Ruth's office.

"Sarge, I checked out those dancers that you wanted us to check into. Janet Chi is dead," JP said.

"What do you mean? How?" Ruth asked.

"What we could find out was that she was beaten to death. The police report also said that she was raped," Robert said and then thinking back to the strange dream that he had.

"So, whoever set up that date with Sharron Jenkins, Janet Chi, and Joshua Pratt, could have killed Janet Chi and maybe Sharron Jenkins," Ruth said.

"How are we going to find out who set the date up?" JP asked.

"I think I am going to give Joshua Pratt a call, maybe he can tell us who he contacted," Ruth said as she picked up the phone.

"Hello, Joshua Pratt's office," said a woman's voice into the phone.

"I would like to speak with Mr. Pratt" Ruth said into the phone

"Please hold and I will see if he is available. Who may say is calling?"

"I am Sergeant Ruth Toshibalua with the Denver Police Department."

"Please hold."

"Hi Ruth...How have you been? It has been a long time since we've spoken or seen you over to the house," a man's voice answered over the phone.

"Hello Joshua, it has been a long time, but this call is about business, it isn't a social call,"

"What can I do for you Ruth?"

"I have something to ask you, and before you answer, I have proof it is you."

"What do you mean? What did I do?"

"About a month ago did you meet a couple of dancers from the Cowboy's Club in a hotel in Black Hawk?"

"Ruth you know me."

"Joshua, I have a video and it shows you. If you don't tell me, I will show it to Caroline"

"Ruth you are my friend so I will level with you. Caroline and I have been having some problems so we decided to see other people at that time. Now we have worked out some of problems and we are staying together for the kids."

"I need to know who set up the date."

"It was some barmaid from the Cowboy's Club."

"Did you get her name?"

"No sorry."

"Okay thank you. Give Caroline and the kids my love, bye," Ruth said into the phone and then hung up.

"He said that it was set up by a barmaid at the Cowboy's Club. He doesn't know her name," Ruth said.

Candy and Megan came back into the office.

"I also need to tell you this, I had a friend in Nashville look up our Mr. Brooks. What she found out was interesting. She found out that Seth Brooks and Sharron Jenkins were husband and wife. Seth was also arrested for beating Sharron up, but Sharron didn't press any charges, so he walked. She also told me that they both have clean records," Ruth said.

"If that's the case, then we could have a spousal murder, and the murderer is dead. So if that is true then we should be really looking at who murdered Seth Brooks," Megan said.

"I need someone to go to Seth Brooks' house and check it out. I will need someone to check out that place Sharron was working at before she came to Colorado. What was the name of that place...Gillian's," Ruth said.

"Why don't Candy and I go," Megan said.

"Okay I'll contact the Nashville police and have them meet you at the house tomorrow. They said that they would help if you needed them," Ruth said.

"That would be great," Megan said and then looked over at Robert who seemed deep in thought. She snapped her fingers in his face to get his attention.

"Yes you go. I will stay here and find out what more about what Seth and Sharron were looking for. I will go undercover as Justin Peterson, Seth's partner at S&J Architecture & Design," Robert said startled.

Chapter 31

Candy pulled the car into the driveway of a red brick house on Willow Springs Drive. Megan noticed the yard was well maintained with ornate shrubs in front of the house. There was a round shaped flower garden in the middle of the yard. She and Candy got out of the car and took out Seth's keys that were in his belongings, and unlocked the front door. They entered the house and closed the door behind them. The entrance led into a large living room with white washed walls and pine wooden floors. The room was furnished with a green sofa and a green matching chair. On the floor was a shag rug under a wooden coffee table. Megan took off her leather jacket and put it on the sofa along with her purse. She looked around the room, before touring the house.

"What do you say we get started? Let's look around and see if we can find any clues to this case," Megan said to Candy who started looking through a writing desk in the corner of the room.

Megan walked into the dining room and then into the living room. She found a room painted light green with pine wooden floors. In the center of the room was a large oak table, with six high back chairs with velvet cushions. On the wall over the buffet table hung a charcoal drawing of a galloping horse in a dark brown wooden frame. She looked through the drawers of the buffet. She found nothing but silverware with the letter B engraved on the silver handles. Beside the silver, there were satin napkins folded in a fashionable style with the letter B stitched into them with gold silk thread. She closed the drawer, and then went on with her search.

"I am going into the kitchen and see what is in there," Candy said as she went through the swinging brown wooden doors, and entered a full kitchen. The walls were painted a bright white. The tile floor matched the white of the walls. In the middle of the kitchen was an island that held a range top. Candy looked through the drawers and cabinets.

"I am going to go look in the bedroom," Megan said when she walked into the kitchen. She noticed everything looked clean and organized.

"Okay, you know this place is just like Sharron Jenkins apartment. Everything clean and very organized, like no one lives here and just a model home for realtors," Candy said.

"Yeah, even the patio is clean of leaves and the grass looks like it was just mowed," Megan said as she looked out the glass doors.

She walked down the narrow, carpeted hall to the back of the house. She came to the bedroom. The walls were painted an off white. The floors were of pine. There was a king size bed in front of a row of windows, at the end of the bed sat a black wooden hope chest. Megan noticed the initials S.J.B engraved on the front in gold letters. She knew that the chest must have belonged to Sharron. She opened the lid but to her dismay found it empty. She closed the lid. She looked around the room and saw a dresser that was resting at the right side of the room. The dresser had six drawers and on top sat an empty jewelry box. At the corner of the dresser was a photo of Sharron. She was dressed in a wedding gown and Seth in a tuxedo.

'Well that proves that Sharron and Seth were married,' she thought to herself. She then went through the drawers of the dresser to see what she could find. She found nothing but a couple of jeans, tops, panties, and bras. Megan looked in the walk in closets and found men's clothes and shoes. She opened the door at the other side of the room and found a small hall. The hall led to a bathroom and another door.

"Megan where are you?"

"I am in the Master bathroom."

Megan opened the door at the end of the bathroom and came to the home office. Candy came into the office in back of her.

"Looks like we found the home office. It looks like the file room at the police station," Megan said as she looked at Candy.

Megan went to the file cabinets next to the door. She opened the first drawer and found it full of folders. Then she opened the other drawers and found them also full of folders. She realized that going through all this would take them forever.

"Candy I think we're going to need some help."

Chapter 32

"Hello, I am Justin Peterson with S&J Architecture & Design. I need some building permits and contracts," Robert said.

"Hello, Mr. Peterson. I am Clark. What building contracts and permits are you looking for?"

"I am looking for the paperwork for the Cowboy's Club. My partner Seth Brooks left the plans, blueprints, and the permits at our Nashville office. So we need a copy of them to finish the job," Robert replied.

"And what is the address of the Cowboy's Club?"

Robert gave Clark the address.

"Okay, I just need to see to verify any plans to remodel or change the building in any way," Clark said as he looked up the address in his computer.

"Yes, I have two remodels, one on the Cowboy's Club. They want to remodel the stage and the bar area," Clark said.

"Could you print out the files? We need to finish this job."

"Well, I would, but you see, Seth Brooks has signed all the paperwork. I need him or the Nashville office to verify that I can give them to you."

"He is at a meeting right now, that's why I am here."

"I will have to call the number he has on the paperwork," Clark said as he called the number.

"Sarge, I found some more information about Victor Marshall. It seems that Victor and Sharron had an intimate relationship. I found multiple emails to Seth Brooks from Sharron Jenkins telling him that Victor Marshall was beating her up," JP said as he handed her the printouts of the emails.

"So, this makes Victor Marshall our prime suspect and he was the last one to see Sharron Jenkins alive," Ruth said as she looked at the emails.

"Yes, you would think that, but Victor has an alibi," JP said.

"Check Mr. Brooks' belongings and find out if you can find more information to the case," Ruth said.

JP went back to his desk and picked up Seth's box of belongings and found his cell phone. He went through the phone text messages, when the phone began to ring. JP answered the call.

"Hello" JP said into the phone.

"Hello could I speak with Seth Brooks please?" Clarks said into the phone.

"Yes, this is Seth Brooks"

"I am Clark Jackson. I am calling you from the Denver Colorado Development Services at the City Hall. Mr. Brooks, I'm calling you because a Justin Peterson is here. He is asking for copies of the paperwork for the Cowboy's Club. Mr. Peterson said that he is your business partner, I need you to verify that for me."

"Yes, he is. I sent him in my place. I was called out of town, so he will be finishing the job."

"It says in the paperwork that you have signed all of the contracts and you have all of the blueprints."

"Yes we do, but I have left them at our Nashville office so I give my permission for you to copy them for Mr. Peterson. Will that be all?"

"Yes, thank you, that is all that I needed."

"Okay bye," JP said smiling to himself at his clever acting and then hung up and went back to the text messages.

Clark looked at Robert and then hung up the phone.

"I have Mr. Brooks' permission to give you the paperwork," Clark said before leaving his desk.

"Thank you," Robert said, wondering what just happened.

When Robert left the Development Services office he called the Cowboy's Club to set up a meeting with Mark Willis.

"Hello, is this Mr. Willis" Robert said into his cell phone.

"Yes, what can I do for you?" Mark said.

"My name is Justin Peterson. I am Mr. Brooks' business partner."

"Mr. Brooks is not here. He will be here tomorrow."

"Mr. Willis the reason I am calling you is that Seth was called out of town on personal business. I will be finishing the job."

"Do you have all the paperwork?"

"Yes, I have the blueprints and the permits that you signed."

"Can you come by around eight tomorrow morning?"

"Yes, I can meet you then. Good bye," Robert said into the phone and then hung up.

It was eight in the morning when the surveillance van pulled up to Gonzales on 950 Colfax. Robert adjusted his tie where the wire and microphone were sewn in.

"Give me a check," JP said as he put his headphones on to see if the microphone was working.

"Check, check, check," Robert said.

"Everything works. Good luck. Here, these glasses will show me what you see. There is a small surveillance camera in the frame just press this button and the camera is turned on, press it again and it is off."

"JP, remember no matter what happens, don't blow my cover. I'm a big boy and can take care of myself," Robert said.

"I understand Robert. I'll let it play out. But if I hear shots, I'm coming in."

"Ok, but only if you hear shots, got it?"

"Roger that."

Robert put on the glasses and then got out of the van. He walked across the street to the Cowboy's Club. He knocked on the door, but there was no answer.

"Hello Mr. Willis it's Justin Peterson...I am outside at the side door," Robert said into his cell phone and then hung up.

"Hello, I am Mark Willis," Mark said after he opened up the door to the club.

"Hello Mr. Willis. I'm Justin Peterson."

"Nice to meet you Mr. Peterson, but please call me Mark and I will call you Justin. Did you bring the blueprints that Seth made out for me?"

"Yes, I have everything in my briefcase," Robert said as he walked over to the bar, and then took out the blueprints and showed them to Mark.

"I was thinking of making a smaller stage for the girls, because our star dancer has the center stage."

"Ok, we can do that. Is that your star? What a beautiful billboard," Robert said as he wrote all the changes that Mark wanted on a notepad.

"Yes, that is our Dancing Star, Crystal Stone. Seth and I were talking about putting a billboard over the center stage also."

"Ok, but why not put her name in neon lights instead of another billboard of her."

"Seth mentioned that also, but you see, every month we change our Star dancer. When that Star Dancer is done for the month, we raffle off the billboard and have her autograph it for them."

"We can put the billboard in a glass case with neon lights around it. Her name can be over the case in neon lights. When you need to change it all you have to do is open the case, and change the letters in the lights."

"I can see that. Let's go with that. I would also like to do something with the girl's dressing room. We are thinking of having male dancers to bring some ladies in for ladies nights," Mark said when they got to the dressing rooms behind the stage.

"Maybe have separate changing room stalls, like they have in the stores at the mall. Is that what you had in mind?"

"That would work, and then have this part be a make-up area. That is a great idea. I want the star dancers to have their own dressing rooms. We need surveillance cameras in all the dressing rooms and also the stalls," Mark said as they went down the hall into the next room.

'It's strange that Mark seems not to trust his dancers.' Robert thought as he followed Mark down the hall to another room.

"This is Sophia's office. She told me that she would like to have more room in here, and maybe add a file room also," Mark said as he went over to the desk picking up a sketch. Then he handed the sketch to Robert who looked at it.

"That is her idea on how she would like the office to look," Mark said.

"Ok. I think we can do this. I will give you some ideas on how we can add a file room in here. I will make a sketch and you tell me what you think."

"That would be great. Down that hall you will find the dressing room of our Star Dancer and the private dancing rooms. I would also like to add a private party room with a small stage. See what you can come up with. I have some paper work in my office I have to do. I will be downstairs if you need me."

"When we start work, where can we put the new furniture and supplies we get?"

"I will show you," Mark said as they walked down the hall to a door with the sign 'fire exit' lit at the top of a door. When they were outside Robert followed Mark across a narrow alley way into another building.

"This is my warehouse," Mark said opening the door. Robert looked around the room was a large room with a dumpster and cardboard boxes in the corner.

"Ok, this will be a great place to store everything," Robert said as he followed Mark back to the club.

File Cabinets

Megan found a folder labeled bills, another one that had the label Sharron Jenkins-Brooks. She pulled the file out of the file cabinet and took it over to the desk and looked through it.

"I think I may have found something, Candy. I found a folder titled Sharron Jenkins-Brooks," Megan said as she opened the folder.

"I found Sharron's birth certificate. It says here that Sharron's name is Tabatha Sharron Jenkins. She was born in Lexington, Kentucky on June 6, 1986. Her mother's name is Helen Marie Underwood, her father Aaron Shawn Jenkins," Megan said as she read the certificate to Candy who wrote the information down on a notepad.

"Here is Seth and Sharron's marriage license," Candy said looking through the file also.

"Here are their divorce papers. I am going to start two piles: important to the case and unimportant," Megan said.

"I found some doctor bills and medical reports. I think we need to look more into it."

"Here is Sharron's paperwork from that place she worked at Gillian's. I think one of us should check it out while we are here."

"Ok, you take the car and go check it out. I am going to stay here and go through all these files," Candy said still looking through the files they had on the desk.

"I will be back to pick you up."

"No need, I will take a cab back to the hotel when I am done here," Candy said.

Robert Is Left Alone

"I also would need a surveillance camera in this office," Mark said before he left Robert to do his work.

Robert waited until Mark left the room before he put in his earpiece so he could hear JP.

"Ok I am in Sophia's office," Robert said and then turned on the camera that was in his glasses frame.

"Find the server tower, it should be in the closet in the back of the room," JP said.

Robert opened the closet door and there was a computer tower and computer screen. He turned on the computer.

"I found the computer, but I need the ID and password to get into it,"

"The ID is all lower case and no spaces cowboygirls. The password is the number twelve, the at sign the number sign, lower case my capital G lower case irls capital J, and the and sign, capital MW. Let me know when you have that typed into the computer," JP said.

"Ok now it is showing me the desk top...wait a minute," Robert said taking out the ear piece and then turning off the camera.

"Hey I am going to go get something to eat. You want anything?" Mark asked as he came into the room.

"No. It looks like I am going to be here a while. I was thinking of making this office brighter, and also enlarging it. Maybe taking out this closet and putting the door about a foot down towards the end of the room."

"That would be great. I will be about an hour, I will let you know when I come back," Mark said and then he left.

Robert put his earpiece back into his ear and turned the camera back on.

"JP, Mark is going out to eat," Robert said.

"I see him. He is crossing the street now," JP said.

"What do we need in the computer?"

"You need to find a server that is all lower case cowboysclubmw. Go through and find anything you can about a client list and anything about Sharron Jenkins or Seth Brooks,"

"Ok this is going to take a while."

"Well, let's hope that Mark Willis is a slow eater."

Robert copied all the files on his external hard drive that he had in his briefcase.

"Robert, are you done?" JP asked an hour later.

"No, why?"

"Mark Willis just left the restaurant."

"It is going to be at least another few minutes."

"Hurry, he is at the crosswalk waiting for the traffic light."

"I have to wait for the computer to finish. I have to erase the memory and then log out."

"He is crossing the street now."

"I am erasing the last hour of the servers memory now...I hear someone coming in."

JP heard Mark's voice and then he heard a loud crash before the microphone went out.

Gillian's

Megan walked into the bar and sat down.

"Hello, can I help you?" asked a tall, slender, red haired woman who was standing behind the bar.

"Hello, I am looking for the owner," Megan said as she looked at the woman.

"You are looking at her, I am Gillian. Are you looking for a job?"

"No, I am Megan Sapphire," Megan said and then showed Gillian her identification.

"What can I do ya for?"

"Did you employ a Sharron Jenkins about five months ago?"

"Yeah, sure. What a sweet kid and a great singer. She sure brought in the crowd."

"When was the last time you saw or spoke to her?"

"Oh, I would say about three months ago. She called and asked me for a reference to work in some club in Denver. Was happy to give her one. I would do anything to keep her away from that no good husband of hers."

"What do you mean?"

"She would come in here with bruises, black eyes, and fat lips almost every night. I would get out the theatrical make-up to cover them before she went on stage. I begged her to leave him, but she always went back to him at the end of her shift...So what is going on? Did she get into some kind of trouble?"

"No. I am sorry to tell you this..,"

"She's dead right?" Gillian interrupted before Megan could finish her sentence.

"Yes she is."

"Well, he definitely done it."

"What do you mean?"

"Sharron left after the divorce papers were signed. I took her to the lawyer. Seth took her for all she had. Sharron was the last of the Jenkins family. They were a famous singing group here in Nashville. When her mom and dad was alive they were known as the Mulberries."

"Wait...what? My mother and father took me to see them when I was young. The little girl was..."

"Yep, that was Sharron, that is why I hired her to sing here."

"Wow, I didn't know that."

"Well, that Seth was a no good rascal. He ran up all kinds of bills. When she divorced him, he kept saying she owed him some money."

"What did she do?"

"I thought she went back to him, because I saw her with him and they seemed happy and all lovey-dovey. I guess she decided that she was going to Denver instead of staying with him."

"Thank you for your time, here is my card if you remember anything else," Megan said as handed Gillian her business card.

Megan called Ruth to let her know what Gillian said.

"Hi Ruth, its Megan," Megan said into her cell phone when Ruth answered.

"Hello Megan, what did you find?"

"Well we found that Seth and Sharron were divorced...Gillian said that Seth beat Sharron. Candy found medical records and police reports, but she never pressed any charges."

"Did you find Sharron's parents?"

"They're dead, but I did find out that they were in a band called the Mulberries. I have one of their records. I will let you listen to it when I get back."

"Ok, keep me informed if you and Candy find out anything more," Ruth said and then hung up.

Megan hung up and called Robert's cell phone. She waited for him answer the phone, but only received his voice mail.

Chapter 33
Inside the Mirror

Megan meditated on Robert's whereabouts. She could see him and feel him. This meditation was different than the rest. She could feel his feelings and hear his thoughts.

He dropped Crystal off at her apartment and then he felt like an evening snack. He got out of the car and walked down a dark alley on Colfax.

"Hey mister, you want to have some fun with us?" asked a thin, blonde woman dressed in a short dress that showed her white lace panties, bra, and high heels.

Robert went over to the woman and her friend, a tall thin black woman also in a short dress and heels. He noticed that the white girl looked like a junky that needed a fix. He went to the black woman and pulled her to his body and smelled her neck. He could tell that she was clean and she would be good to feed on. The other girl he would just strangle to death before he fed. He let the black woman go and walked over to the blonde.

"Come with me," Robert said to the white woman as he grabbed her by the wrist and then pulled her into a building after opening the door. When they were inside the building he took off the woman's bra and as she was taking off her panties. Robert put the bra around the woman's neck and put his hand over her mouth to stifle her screams. He held the woman close to him he leaned on the closed door to stop the other woman from coming in. He pulled the bra with his mouth and his hand while the woman tried to kick and fight for life. Robert could feel her heart beating faster as her breathing went into flight or fight mode. He could feel the woman's life slipping away as she grew weaker in her fight. When he pulled the bra again around the woman's slender neck until her body went limp and then he took the bra from around her neck. The he snapped her neck so he knew that she was dead.

Robert put the woman's dead body into a dumpster beside the door and then took off his clothes. All the while he held the door closed with his foot. He then let go of the door so the other woman would come in.

The black woman busted into the building and looked around for her friend.

"What did you do with her?" The woman asked as she looked frantically around the room.

"She is sleeping. I wore her out. We will wake her when we are done."

He took the woman into his arms and ripped off her bra. He then looked at her dark skin and softly kissed her big brown breasts. He took each of her nipples into his mouth as he licked and gently bit them one at a time. He reached his hand into her panties and found that she was wet.

"MMMM....," she moaned at his touch.

"You like that do you?"

"Yes...oh fuck yeah."

"I am going to rip these panties off of you and then bend you over and fuck the shit out of you," Robert said as he ripped her panties off of her body. He reached between them and began to pleasure her with his hand.

"I want you to fuck me and make me your bitch!" she moaned.

"You do, then bend the fuck over and take it like the whore that you are," Robert said as he pushed her down and she grabbed her ankles. He entered her and began to fuck her. He grabbed her long black hair and pulled her up to him. He then pushed her onto her hands and knees onto the cement floor and entered her again. When he could not take it anymore, he pulled her head and neck up to him. He licked the side of her brown neck and tasted the saltiness of her sweat. The taste made him excited and he pushed himself deeper and harder into her. He held her neck and then he bit into the salty flesh until he tasted the sweetness of her clean blood. The woman screamed in pain as he sucked her now bloody neck. As he fucked her harder and faster like a crazed animal. When he spilled his seed into her he could hear the drumming inside his head. He let go when the drumming of the woman's heart became weak.

Robert walked down the alleyway toward the gathering club. He sensed someone following close behind him. He could hear the click of the heavy heels hitting the pavement of the sidewalk behind him. He could hear their breath and the person smelled of a man. Robert walked faster as the man closed in on him.

"Hey you!" called a man's voice.

"What?" Robert stopped and came face to face with a hefty black man.

"Did you see two whores in this alleyway about an hour ago?"

"No."

"I think you did," the black man said and took a gun out of his jacket. He pointed the gun at Robert...

Mirror

Megan was awoken by the ringing of the phone. She looked at the alarm clock to see what time it was. The clock read six in the morning.

"Who can be calling at this time of the morning?" Megan asked answering her cell phone.

"Hello?"

"Hi Megan, it is Ruth."

"Oh, Ruth."

"You sound sleepy did I wake you?"

"No, I was getting up anyway."

"Have you heard from Robert?"

"No I haven't, why?"

"He was supposed to meet us here this morning, but we haven't heard from him. Oh, and Mark Willis called Ellie's house looking for you, he wants you to call him."

"I will call him."

"Call me back."

"Ok, I will call you back," Megan said and then hung up the phone and then made another call.

"Hello Cowboy's Club?" Mark's said into the phone.

"Hi Mark, it's Nina."

"Hello Nina, I called to see if you could come in tonight and work."

"I can't. I am busy for the next few days."

"Nina my love, you want the job still don't you."

"Yes, I still want the job,"

"Well, I need you tonight, if you don't come in you will lose the job."

"Ok, I will see you tonight," Megan said into the phone and then hung up and called Ruth back.

"Hi Ruth, I need to fly back to Denver this morning."

"Why? What is going on?"

"Mark wants me to start dancing tonight."

"OK, have Candy go through Seth Brooks' house. I will call my friend at the Nashville Police department and have her help."

"Great, I'll see you this afternoon. Could you have JP call the airport and change my ticket for me? I am going to go check out that place that Sharron worked for."

"Can I speak with Candy?"

"She stayed at Seth's last night. She was going through the file cabinets."

"Have her give me a call."

"I will. Hey Ruth, have someone or JP look on Colfax in the warehouse next to the Cowboy's club for Robert."

"Why?"

"I don't know, just a hunch. Call me back and let me know," Megan said as she remembered her dream that she had about Seth Brooks the night before he died. Now she thought about the dream she had about Robert last night.

Chapter 34

"Hello. I am officer Joanna Sparks," said a tall thin busty black woman walking up to Megan's rental car.

"Yes, you must be Ruth's friend. I am Megan Sapphire. I am so glad you are helping us out, because I have to fly back to Denver today. My partner will be staying here and she can use some help," Megan said as she walked up to the front door of the house with Joanna.

"What do you need help with?"

"We need to know if Seth Brooks was capable or had any motive for murdering his estranged wife. We need some help going through their files and computers. We also need to question the neighbors about the Brooks' home life."

"We do have reports that Mrs. Brooks called the police on Mr. Brooks for domestic violence. No charges were filed. She would just tell us that he needed to leave."

"Could you please fax that report and anything else your department has to Ruth? That would be helpful, and thank you for your help Officer Sparks," Megan said as they went into the house. Joanna followed her down the hall to the home office.

"Candy this is Officer Joanna Sparks, she will be helping you go through all these files. I have to go back to Denver today," Megan said to Candy who was sitting on the floor with open folders around her.

"Are these the files?" Joanna asked when she saw the file cabinets.

"Thank you for your help Officer Sparks. Yes, these are the files, we need to go through every folder," Candy said as she looked up at Megan and Joanna.

"I will help as much as I can before I have to leave," Megan said as she opened one of the file cabinets.

"Okay where do I start? And please call me Joanna," Joanna said as she took a folder out and made her way to the desk.

"We have already started. We do need to get a computer expert to go through the computers," Megan said as walked to the desk and sat next to Joanna.

"Well we are in luck, I majored in computer science in college," Joanna said.

"Great, you can work on the computer and we will work on the files," Candy said.

"I need to call JP and find out when my plane leaves," Megan said and as she got up from her chair and left the room.

"This is JP's phone, JP speaking," JP answered when he picked up the phone.

"Hi JP, it's Megan."

"Hey Megan, how are you?"

"I am doing fine. Did you call the airlines and change my plane ticket?"

"Yes I did, your flight is at eleven thirty-five this morning. Your flight is two hours and forty-five minutes so that will put you at the Denver airport at ten thirty-five Denver time."

"Okay, I have a couple of hours before I have to get to the airport,"

"Okay Megan, I will pick you up at the airport."

"Did you hear anything from Robert?"

"No, not yet."

"Did you check out the warehouse that I told Ruth about?"

"No, but I will."

"Why don't you do that instead of picking me up? I will ask Candy if I can use her jeep."

"Ok, I will see you when you get back."

"Megan, we found some interesting things on this computer. Come take a look," Candy yelled to her from the office.

"I will be right there," Megan yelled back, taking the phone away from her ear.

"JP, I will see you at the station when I get back to Denver. I have to go now, bye," Megan said into the phone and then hung up. She went back into the office to see what Joanna and Candy wanted to show her.

"Candy, can I use your jeep when I get back to Denver?" Megan asked coming into the room.

"Sure," Candy said.

"So, what did you need to show me?" Megan asked looking at the computer over Joanna's shoulder.

"Well, I don't know if this means anything to you. But here is a file with all the ID's and passwords to all the files of the Cowboy's Club's computers. Now here is a file of the information of the Denver bank accounts, paychecks of the employees, and the stock information for the Cowboy's Club," Joanna said clicking on the folder and opening the contents. Megan read the contents of the folder and skimmed through the files. There were bank accounts for Mark Willis and all the information and social security numbers of all the employees. All the passwords and ID's of the Cowboy's Club server and computer files. Megan could not believe all the information that was there.

"It looks like Seth and Sharron were planning to blackmail Mark Willis and the Cowboy's Club. Candy, remember the video that was in the briefcase that was in the safety deposit box at the bank?"

"Yeah, what about it?"

"Janet told Sharron to give her some money, so that she could pay the person that set up the date for them. I wonder if it was Mark Willis that set up that date," Megan said thinking out loud.

"You know, I bet you are right," Candy said raising her eyebrows.

"I need these files printed or saved on a flash drive so I can take them back to Denver with me," Megan said and then looked through the drawers of the desk.

Chapter 35

When Megan got to the airport she called Robert's cell phone.

"Hello this is Detective Robert Towers. I can't get to the phone, so leave a message," Robert's voice said over the phone.

"Hello Robert, it's Megan. I am heading back to Denver, give me a call when you get this," Megan said into the phone and then hung up.

When she picked up her ticket, she found out that JP had her in first class.

"I am going to have JP book all my flights from now on," she said to herself as she got on the plane and went to her seat.

"Hello I am Kathy. I will be your flight attendant. Can I get you anything while we are still boarding the plane?"

"Yes I'll have a glass of Merlot please," Megan replied and then smiled.

She waited until Kathy left to get her wine before she took the folder out of her bag. She opened the file and pawed through the paperwork and documents inside. She found Sharron's birth certificate and Sharron's and Seth's marriage license and certificate. She took out a notepad out of her purse. She noted that Seth was from Pigeon Forge, Tennessee. Sharron was from Lexington, Kentucky. They were married February 2, 2012 in Nashville, Tennessee. She noticed the priests name was Father Jacob Marigold and the witnesses were Helen Marie Jenkins and Loretta May Brooks, both Sharron and Seth's mothers. She was still looking at the marriage certificate when the flight attendant brought her wine. Megan drank her wine as she looked through the other documents in the folder.

"Ladies and gentlemen this is your captain speaking. We will be leaving Nashville in a couple of moments and heading to Denver, Colorado. The flight will be two hours and forty-five minutes. We are just waiting for the okay to start down the runway before we can take off. Just sit back relax and enjoy the flight."

After Megan finished her wine, she sat the file aside on the empty seat next to her. She closed her eyes and let her mind wander. She couldn't help but think about Robert and first time they met...

"Megan this is your new partner Officer Robert Towers," Ruth said introducing them for the first time.

"Sarge is there someone else that you can partner me up with? She is a woman not a police officer," Robert said looking at Megan who was glaring at him.

"Officer Sapphire, why don't you show Officer Towers what you can do with a firearm," Ruth said and then gave a sly smirk.

Megan and Ruth took Robert to the shooting range down stairs of the police station, to prove that she could shoot.

"Officer Towers, do you see that target over there? The one over there, and there?" Megan asked as she took her revolver out of her hip holster. She pointed her gun at the targets and shot all three, within seconds, hitting all of them.

"Yeah well, let's see if you hit the bull's eye or missed," Robert said and then gave a sly smirk.

"JP, bring the targets up so we can see if I hit them," Megan called.

When the targets were in front of them, they saw that Megan hit the bull's eye on everyone.

Robert looked at the targets. He could not believe that she had hit them all so fast.

"Officer Sapphire is a master in weaponry. She was trained by the best. Officer Towers before you judge a person by their gender get to know what they are capable of doing," Ruth scolded...

Megan awoke to the sound of the captain's voice.

"Ladies and gentlemen, I have turned on the fasten seat belts sign. We are in a pocket of turbulence. We will be out of it soon."

Megan let her mind wonder as she looked out the window...

"I would like to take the time to announce the promotion of Officer Megan Sapphire and Officer Robert Towers. They are promoted from officers to detectives, we are so proud of them," Sergeant Ruth Toshibalua said over the microphone.

Megan and Robert were now detectives for the Denver Police Department. Megan could not believe it. She thought about her parents. She wished that they were alive to see her get her promotion.

"Meg, are you ok?" Robert asked when he saw tears roll down her face. When she walked over and stood next to him.

"Yeah I am fine. I wish my parents could be here," she said as she wiped her tears away.

After the promotion ceremony, the governor had a get together at his mansion for all the new detectives.

"You look lovely, detective," Robert said when he walked over to Megan admiring her red knee length silk dress.

"Hello detective, you're looking handsome. I didn't know that you cleaned up so well," Megan said also complementing Robert on the dark blue suit.

"It seems that you two have come far since I decided to make you partners. See, I knew I was right pairing you two up," Ruth said and then winked at them.

"Yes, I can't believe I ever doubted you Sarge," Robert said and then smiled at her.

"I wanted to congratulate you both. You two have fun. I am going to go talk to the Governor," Ruth said before she left them.

"So… tell me what made you want to become a detective and police officer?" Robert asked Megan.

"Well it is a long story, but I wanted to be a traffic cop. My parents were killed in a hit and run accident by a drunk driver," Megan said as her eyes got watery, but she would not allow the tears to fall.

"I am sorry to hear that Meg," Robert said as he put his arm over her shoulder to comfort her.

"Well, that is when I decided that I had to do my best to keep drunk drivers off the roads. So what made you want to be a cop and detective?"

"Well my parents were police officers. I guess it's in my blood."

"Were they at the ceremony today?"

"No, they were not. They were killed by two bank robbers in Miami. My parents were trying to save the hostages, and the robbers killed everyone in the bank, along with my parents," Robert said sorrowfully.

"I am sorry to hear that Robert."

"Ladies and Gentlemen, we are about to ready to descend to our destination. I will be turning on the fasten seat belt sign in a few moments," the Captain said over the speaker.

Chapter 36

"Megan welcome back, did you find anything in Nashville?" Ruth asked when Megan came into her office.

"Yes, we found out that Sharron and Seth were planning to blackmail the Cowboy's Club and Mark Willis," Megan said and then the flash drive out of her purse and gave it to Ruth.

"What's on this?"

"All of the plans. Also, the bank accounts for the Mark Willis and the employees. This is Sharron's and Seth's marriage certificate, Sharron's birth certificate and medical records," Megan said as she handed Ruth the folder. Ruth took the folder and looked through it.

"What are these medical records?"

"It seems that Seth was abusive to Sharron when they were married."

"Yes, you said that when you called,"

Ruth was looking at the report when her phone rang.

"Hello, this is Sergeant Ruth Toshibalua, what can I help you with," Ruth said when she answered the phone.

"Hi. sergeant, it's Candy, did Megan get back ok?"

"Yes. she did."

"Well. that is great to hear, did she show you what we found?"

"Yes, but I haven't had a chance to look at the flash drive," Ruth said and then put the flash drive into her computer to look at the files.

"Are you looking at it now?"

"Yes."

"They are plans for the Cowboy's Club. I am going to send you some files. Did JP get a chance to talk to Sophia Mark Willis' secretary yet?"

"I have not heard anything yet."

"Sarge, did you get the files?"

"Yes, they are uploading now."

Ruth opened the files. She read the emails from Sharron to Seth about how they were going to blackmail the club. Sharron was going to go from dancer to star dancer. In the meantime she would become friends with Crystal Stone the star dancer. Seth had fake modeling and acting contracts drawn up for her. He told her to show them to Mark and Sophia as proof that she would be a great asset to the club.

"Is that all you found out so far?"

"Yes, I will call you if we find anything else," Candy said and then hung up.

"Hey Sarge, I am back. Oh hey Megan, good to see you're back. I have a surprise for both of you," JP said when he came into the office.

"Hello, what is it?" Ruth asked.

"It is me!" Robert said when he came into the office.

"Where the hell were you? You had us worried sick that your cover was blown or worse," Ruth said in a scolding tone to her voice.

"Mark wanted me to start work right away," Robert replied in his own defense.

"Why didn't you answer your cell phone? All of us have been trying to call you," Megan said as she glared at him.

"My cell phone battery was out of juice," Robert confessed.

"Megan, guess where I found him?" JP asked and then laughed.

"Where?...not where I said to look for him?" Megan asked

"You must be some kind of friggin' Psychic. He was in the warehouse by the club," JP said.

"Ok now that is settled, what did you find at the Cowboy's Club?" Ruth asked as she looked at Robert.

"Well here is the flash drive," Robert said as he took the flash drive out of his briefcase and then handed it to Ruth. She put the drive into her computer. Ruth got up from her chair and let Robert sit down to access her computer.

"Well, this is an email from Mark to Sophia asking her if she thought that Sharron Jenkins should be the next star dancer," Robert said as he opened the email.

"Oh yes, that reminds me JP, has Sophia returned yet?" Ruth asked looking over at JP.

"I haven't heard from her, yet," JP said.

"JP, just to be on the safe side, you should see if you can keep an eye on Crystal Stone and also Sophia. I have Mark Willis and Victor Marshall covered," Megan said.

"That is a great idea," Ruth said.

"Ok, I will give Crystal a call and see what she is doing tonight," JP said.

"This is an email to Victor Marshall from Sophia explaining that they had a new dancer Sharron Jenkins. This one is from Sharron to

Sophia asking her if Crystal Stone was looking for a roommate. Sophia's response was yes, but she thought Crystal would not be keen on the idea since Sharron was taking her place as the new star dancer for the club. This email from Sophia to Victor has been deleted," Robert said.

Just then JP's cell phone rang. He left the room to take the call.

"I just got a call from Mark Willis. He said Sophia is back in town, and that she will be at the club in an hour. He also gave me her cell number," JP said when he came back into the room.

"Okay, go speak with Sophia. In the meantime, I am going to call and see if we can view the surveillance tapes from the Sheraton Hotel's garage," Ruth said.

Chapter 37

When JP got to the Cowboy's club he knocked on the back entrance door, but there was no answer. He called Sophia on her cell phone.

"Hi..Sophia it's JP..I am at the door," JP said into the phone and then hung up.

The door was opened by a tall woman with straight, shoulder length blonde hair. Sophia was a slender middle aged woman. She reminded him of Marilyn Monroe wearing a low cut top. JP could not help but admire her curves.

"Hello, I am Sophia Abbott," Sophia said shaking hands with JP. She noticed that this handsome man was taking off her clothes with his eyes. She didn't mind because men always loved to stare at her cleavage.

"I am sorry for staring but..I mean..I am JP... it is nice to meet you."

"Nice to meet you too, JP. I have the files that you asked about, but there is not much in them. I also have Sharron's application, her evaluation, and also her promotion application," Sophia said as she locked the door and went to the bar with JP who followed behind.

"Sophia, do you know what happened to Sharron after she left here?" JP asked looking at Sharron's job application.

"No."

"It says that Sharron was working for Martha's Cafe before she worked here," JP said he as took his notepad out of his pocket to jot down the information. "Did you know Sharron Jenkins well?"

"No I didn't. The only time I spoke with her is when she needed to sign contracts or I needed to talk to the dancers," Sophia answered.

"Okay, I need to know what you can tell me about Victor Marshall," JP said as he noticed how Sophia bit her bottom lip and crinkled her eyebrows in a worried look.

"Victor Marshall? Why do you need to know about him?" She asked in a shaky voice.

"Victor Marshall was the last known person to see Sharron Jenkins alive. I would like to know if he would have any motive for wanting her dead," JP said as he wondered what Sophia had to hide.

"Mark said that you wanted to know about Sharron Jenkins, he didn't say anything about Victor," Sophia said and then she shook like she was cold.

"I didn't tell him everything that I wanted to ask you. Can you tell me more about Victor?"

"Victor Marshall would have no cause to kill Sharron. I can vouch for that. I know him."

"How well do you know him?"

"He and I used to date."

"Do you know where he was Saturday morning, June the twentieth?"

"June the twentieth....mmm... he was giving me a ride to the airport."

"What time was your flight?"

"My flight was seven in the morning. He picked me up after his shift."

"What time did Mr. Marshall pick you up?"

"He came to my apartment at around six in the morning," Sophia said with a look on her face like she was trying to remember the answer to a question on a test.

"I have a few more questions for you. What can you tell me about Seth Brooks?"

"Sharon recommended him to remodel the club. I know that he started the job, and then he was called out of town. Now, I believe his business partner, a Mister...Peterson, I think that is his name. Hold on I will go and get his information," Sophia said and then left JP at the bar while she went to get the information.

"Here you go. His name is Justin Peterson. I have not had time to check him out yet. Mark did tell me that he came by with all the plans and contracts," Sophia said when she returned from her office. JP looked at the information that they had so far on Robert's undercover identity.

"Hey, maybe he killed Sharron Jenkins," Sophia said sarcastically.

"Maybe, we can go over everything at dinner tonight?"

"I would, but I have work to do, maybe some other time."

"Tomorrow night?"

"That would be nice. Now if there is nothing else, I really should get back to my work."

"No, I think that is all for now. I will call you tomorrow," JP said and then followed Sophia to the door so he could leave.

After JP left Sophia made a call on her cell phone.

"Hi we need to talk...Tonight meet me at my house...we need to make some plans," she said into the phone and then hung up.

"I am so glad you called me," Crystal said.

"I thought that we could go out and talk," JP said.

"About what?"

"I would like to get to know you."

"Hi, I am Timothy I will be your waiter," a freckled teenage kid said when he came to their table.

"I would like a summer salad and a diet coke," Crystal said

"I will have a hamburger with a coke," JP said.

Timothy took their orders and left to get the food.

"So why did you ask me out to lunch?"

"Well, I must confess, since the time I saw you at Valentines', I wanted to meet you."

"That must have been when I was doing the motorcycle promotion."

"I think it was a motorcycle show. I saw you dance and thought you were beautiful."

Timothy came back with their food.

"Do you still dance there?" JP asked as he put ketchup on his burger.

"I do, when they need me,"

"So Valentines' and the Cowboy's Club are partners?"

"You could say that. Mark and the owner of Valentines' are step brothers."

"I see."

JP and Crystal ate their meals, when they were finished JP drove Crystal to the Cowboy's Club.

Chapter 38

"Mark, thank you for taking me out to dinner," said Megan.

"Nina, it is my pleasure. I think I am going to have the lobster," Mark said as he looked at his menu.

"That sounds good, but I think I will have the chicken," Megan said as she put down her menu.

"No, you will have the lobster also," Mark said and then waved the waiter over to their table.

"Yes Mr. Willis, are you ready to order?" asked the waiter.

"Yes, I will have the lobster and the lady will have the same," Mark said.

"So tell me Nina, how do you like Colorado so far?" Mark asked when the waiter left the table.

"I haven't seen much of Colorado, just Denver," Megan lied.

"Well, we will have to change that real soon. By the way I was thinking of going to Black Hawk tonight. Why don't you come along?"

"I thought you needed me to dance tonight at the club."

"Well, I am the boss. So if you are with me, you are working,"

"I see."

"Ah, our food is here,"

"Will that be all Mr. Willis?" the waiter asked as he put their plates in front of them.

"We will have your best bottle of champagne," Mark said to the waiter who rushed off to get it.

"Nina I would like to get to know you," Mark said as he placed his hand over Megan's.

"Mark I was hoping that you would say that."

"I would like to introduce you as the new dancer at the car show next week."

"Where is the car show?"

"It is in Black Hawk in Valentines' parking lot."

"Would you excuse me? I have to use the restroom."

"Yes, by all means," Mark said as he got up and pulled out Megan's chair for her. She got up and walked to the restroom in back of the dining room.

When Megan was in the ladies room she called Ruth.

"Hello Ruth, its Megan."

"Hi Megan, what's up?"

"I need you to have Robert check out Valentines' in Black Hawk for me."

"Do you mean Valentines' Casino?"

"I think so."

"That is the only Valentines' in Black Hawk."

"Well anyway, Mark wants me to go there tonight with him. Also he wants me to go there for a car show next week."

"Megan, I thought you were going to dance tonight?"

"I don't know, but he wants me to go with him tonight. I will see you tomorrow. If you don't see or hear from me have Robert call Mark."

"Megan, please be careful."

"You know I will," Megan said and then hung up.

Megan left the ladies room and walked back to the table. Mark got up when he saw her and pulled out her chair for her.

"I took the liberty of pouring you a glass of champagne."

"Thank you," Megan said and picked up the glass and took a sip.

"I was thinking that we could stay in Black Hawk tonight."

"Robert, did you and JP go over the flash drive that Megan brought back from Seth's?" Ruth asked as she looked at the evidence board.

"I am still going over the files. JP went home for the night," Robert said.

"Well, it is getting late. Why don't you go home?" Ruth said as she looked at her wrist watch.

"I do my best work at night, besides I don't sleep all that well."

"I know what you mean. I hate to go home at night, it is too lonely...Robert I want to thank you again for what you did for me in California."

"Don't worry about it Ruth. I just wish I could have brought your daughter home alive."

"I know. You gave up a lot to investigate her murder for me. Did you ever tell Megan the real reason you left?"

"No. I promised you that I wouldn't."

"Just think you and Megan might have been married by now. I owe you so much."

"Ruth, don't worry about it."

"Well Megan is going to Black Hawk she told me when she called. If we don't hear from her tomorrow, she wants you to call Mark."

"Raven, I would like to introduce you to Rocco Valentine," Mark said.

"It is nice to meet you," Megan said.

"It is my pleasure, my dear," Rocco said and then he took Megan's hand in his and kissed it.

Rocco Valentine was a tall, well built man that looked like a younger version of Mark.

"So my brother, I would like to have Raven come and do the car show next week," Mark said.

"Work, always work with you. We can talk about that later. Right now I would like to get to know this Raven beauty that you brought me," Rocco said and then escorted Megan to the bar.

"I am going to go check out your new craps table," Mark said as Rocco waved him away.

"So would you like something to drink?" Rocco asked Megan.

"I will have a red wine," Megan said and then looked around the casino. Rocco gave her the wine and took a scotch and soda for himself.

"Do you gamble?"

"I play a little black jack."

"Would you like to play?"

"I don't have any money," Megan said shyly.

"You don't need money my love. You can play with mine," Rocco said as he walked with Megan to the black jack table.

When Megan was seated at the table Rocco sat next to her as the dealer gave them some gambling chips. He then dealt the cards to them, Megan picked up her cards. She had a king and queen. After she looked at her cards she bet a hundred dollar chip.

"Would you like a hit?" The dealer asked as he looked at Megan.

"I think that I am going to stay with what I have," Megan replied to the dealer and then she looked over at Rocco.

"I am going to have a hit," Rocco said and then smiled at Megan as he also bet. The dealer showed them his cards he had a queen and a three. He laid another card down it was a six.

"The dealer has nineteen," The dealer said and then he turned over Megan's and Rocco's cards.

"The lady has twenty, and the gentleman pushes with the dealer," The dealer said as he gave Megan another hundred dollar chip.

"Well I guess you do play blackjack," Rocco said and then he smiled at Megan.

"I used to play with my father when I was young," Megan said as the dealer dealt another hand.

"He taught you well. So how long have you been working at the Cowboy's Club?"

"I just started," Megan said and then looked at her cards before she made another bet.

"I will stay with these cards," Rocco said after he looked at his cards and bet.

"So do you use the dancers from the club to do shows for your casino?"

"We often use the star dancer from the club when we are doing a promotion for the casino. Crystal Stone did our last television commercial about a month ago. Sharron Jenkins was going to do our next one. It was going to be for the car show."

"How well do you know Crystal? Did you know Sharron well?"

"I have known Crystal since she started working for Mark. Sharron I only met one time."

"Did Sharron do a show for you?"

"No. Crystal comes here and dances on the bar for me twice a month to bring gamblers in. I used to have Janet and Crystal dance on the craps table's stage. So you are Mark's new star dancer. Maybe I will have you do the commercial for me next week."

Chapter 39

When Megan and the other dancers got to Valentines' hotel and casino, they were met by Sophia and Victor Marshall who were waiting for them at the hotel check-in desk.

"Good Morning, Ladies. I would like to welcome you to Valentine's Casino Car Show Weekend. We are going to go, now that everyone is here," Sophia said and then she and Victor escorted the dancers to the parking garage to a van. After they were all in the van they drove to Mark's house.

"Where are we going?" Megan asked.

"We are going to Mark's mountain house, it is not too far," Sophia said.

When they got to the house all the girls and Sophia got out of the van.

"Okay Ladies, after you all are settled in, come down to the pool so we can go over what you will be doing for the car show and over the weekend."

"Raven, I need you to meet with me after. Put your things in your room then I need you to sign some contracts. I will meet you in the library it is down the hall from the living room," Sophia said before she left the porch and then went into the house.

"Rave, we are sharing a room together," Crystal said as they went into the house.

The entryway opened into a big room that had a pine wooden stair case that led to the second floor. Megan looked around the entry room that led to other entry way to other rooms on the first floor of the house, but the rooms could not be seen from the entry room. Megan and the others went up the stairs to their rooms on the second floor.

"This is our room here," Crystal said as she opened the wooden door that led into a room that looked like a living room. It was painted white with white wooden floors. Megan saw two closed doors that she thought could be the bedrooms.

"This is your room and this one is mine," Crystal said as she pointed to the closed door on the right while she opened the door on the left. Megan opened the door and found a large room that held a king size bed in the middle of the room. She put her bags on the bed and looked around the room. The walls and floor were covered in wooden pine. She saw that the room had a bathroom with a full sunk in bath tub, glassed in shower stall and a toilet. The room also had a huge wooden and porcelain vanity. She decided that she would give Robert a call to see if he found anything yet. Also, she wanted to let him know where she was in case anything happened. Before she could make the call, she heard a knock on the bedroom door and then she heard Crystal's voice.

"Rave, we should go and get your contracts signed and go meet the others at the pool. Sophia is a bitch when it comes to being late," Crystal called through the door.

"I will be right there," Megan called back to her.

Megan thought that her call would have to wait until tonight before she went to bed.

Crystal showed Megan the way to the library where Sophia was waiting for her.

"I told you to find it!" Sophia yelled at Victor who was sitting in the leather chair by the desk that Sophia was sitting at.

"I don't know where he has hidden it, but if it is in this house I will find it," Victor said.

"Well you better, or it could mean that we lose everything that…" Sophia said and then looked up to find Megan who was standing in the door way. Sophia shifted nervously in her chair as looked at Victor. Victor turned his head to see what made Sophia so antsy.

"Raven, come in and have a seat," Sophia said pointing to the empty chair that was next to Victor.

"Victor, I believe that we are done for now," Sophia said as she glared at him before he got up and left the room.

"Raven, I just need you to sign some contracts, just stating that all the photos and video that we are going to shoot of you are the property of the Cowboy's Club. Also that you are only a representative of the club and you will have no rights to any of them. This one is to allow us to take photos and video of you. This one is giving us the right to use your video and photos as we see fit," Sophia said as she showed Megan the contracts and explained them before she could sign them. Megan signed them as Nina Keller. After she signed the contracts, Sophia put them in a folder and smiled.

"So Nina, now you are Raven, everyone is going to know you as Raven not Nina Keller," Sophia said.

"Is that all you need me for, Sophia?" Megan asked before got up to leave the room.

"Yes it is, would you go to the pool and tell the girls I will be right out to have the meeting," Sophia said. She waited until Megan left the room before she picked up the phone to make a call.

"Hello...I need you to check a couple people out for me...yes the first name is Justin Peterson from Nashville, Tennessee...the next name is Nina Keller also from Nashville, Tennessee...I will fax you their information...I need all the information that you can find as soon as possible. You can fax it back to me," Sophia said and then hung up the phone and then faxed the information.

Sophia came out of the house and made her way to the pool.

"Thank you ladies, for meeting me here. I just want to go over what is going to happen in the morning and what everyone is going to be wearing," Sophia said as she walked over to the table next to the pool and sat down in one of the chairs next to the table. She took out the instructions from the folder in her hand.

"Okay, let's start with the booths. You will each have a booth at the car show. Next to your booth will be one of the show cars. When people come up to your booth, you will sign one of your promotional photos. We will be taking the photos on the car that is chosen to be your show car. If they ask to have a picture with you, you will then pose with them in front of the car. Any questions so far?" Sophia asked and then looked at the girls.

"I have a question, what will we be wearing?" asked a tall busty brunet girl not much older than twenty one. She was wearing a white tee shirt that showed her nipples and she had on tight jean short shorts.

"Alison, each of you will be wearing one of your costumes. Victor is getting them out of the van and they will be in your rooms when we are done here," Sophia answered with a smile.

"Everyone has signed their contracts for tomorrow's show right?" Sophia asked looking through the folder at the contracts of the dancers.

"Yes you all did. Now enjoy your stay. We will be here for three days and then it is back to Denver. On the third day there will be a party in the honor of the car owners and also the bidders on the cars. The party will be in Valentines' Casino ballroom. That is all. You will find schedules in your rooms of everything that is going on and what you need to do while we are here. So have fun, but remember we are here to work and the schedules need to be kept. So don't be late," Sophia said before she got up from the table and walked back to the house.

Megan decided that now would be a good time to call Robert and let him know what was going on, also to check in on Katie and see how she was doing.

"Rave, all of us are going swimming. Are you going to try out the hot tub and the pool with us?" Crystal asked.

"I think I am going to go swimming, but first I need to get changed and unpack," Megan said as she headed toward the house.

"You didn't put on your swim suit under your tee shirt and shorts?" Alison asked as she took off her shorts and she was wearing blue bikini bottoms.

"You know what is going to happen if you swim in that white tee shirt without a top or a bra under it?" Megan asked as she looked at Alison's breasts.

"Well, that is why I am a stripper. Everyone has seen them. So, I have nothing to hide," Alison said and then laughed as she jumped into the pool.

Sophia looked at the fax machine on the desk when she came back into the library but found nothing there.

"Well, all the costumes are in the girls' rooms. What can I do before I have to go back to Denver?" Victor asked when he came into the library.

"What?" Sophia asked and then looked up at him.

"I put the costumes in the rooms. What do you need me to do now?" Victor asked when he walked over to Sophia and put his arms around her curvy waist.

"Did you find the information from the safe in the wine cellar?" Sophia asked and then gave him a peck on the lips.

"I did, but there was not much there. I think when everyone is asleep tonight I am going to go look in his bedroom for the papers. If the papers are not in this house, then they must be in his house in Las Vegas or maybe at the club."

"No. The papers and books are not there. I looked. That is why I went back to Vegas, to see if he hid them in his vacation house," Sophia said with a look of defeat on her face.

"We will find them my love. Maybe I should get his key to his house in Denver and check there."

"Justin, I like your plans. I think that this place will look great when you're done," Mark said looking at the plans and blueprints.

"Seth told me to show you our plans for the club. He will be out of town longer then he thought. So I am going to hire the crew and do the work for him," Robert said

"Okay, but I want you to make some extra plans and blueprints for my downstairs office. I need a wall safe that is fire proof and theft proof. I also want a hidden room in the back with hidden cameras in the walls."

"What would you like in the room? How do you want it decorated?" Robert asked wondering why Mark would want a hidden room.

"I will let my decorator design the room. All you have to do is worry about creating it."

"Okay, who is going to be here while we are working?"

"No one, the girls and Sophia are going to be in Black Hawk at a car show for three days, and I am going to Las Vegas for a few days. Today is Friday, so no one will be here until next Friday. So that gives you a week to get everything done. Do you have any more questions? Because I am going to the airport after I leave here."

"No, I think that we will be fine,"

"Well if you do, call Sophia. I will leave her number on the bar. Victor will be here tomorrow to clean up and restock the bar, but he won't get in your way."

Chapter 40

Megan found a leather skirt and halter top that zipped up the front laying on the bed. The schedule for the car show was sitting on top of the costume.

"Rave, are you getting ready for lunch? We are going to the photo shoot at Valentines. Victor is going to drive us there," Crystal said coming into the door way of Megan's room before going into her own room to change.

"What are we to wear?" Megan asked hoping that she was not supposed to wear the costume.

"Shorts and the Cowboy's Club tee shirt. It is under the costume on your bed,"

Megan picked up the leather outfit and found a white tee shirt. She picked it up and looked at the logo, a blue rhinestone cowboy hat and inside the hat was written in red cursive letters was 'Cowboy's Club'. She thought that the tee shirt looked kind of tacky, but she took off her tank top and put it on. When she was dressed she came out of her room to find Crystal sitting in the chair talking with Victor. They stopped talking when they saw her.

"Damn, girl you look hot as hell," Victor said when he saw her.

"Okay, I am ready, let's go, I'm starving," Megan said and then smiled.

"Did you find anything on the information that I faxed to you?...No I will be back this evening...okay then, I will call you back tomorrow morning," Sophia said into her cell phone before she hung up. 'I finished the conversation just in time,' Sophia thought to herself when she saw the girls coming into the library.

"Okay girls, you all look great. We are going to Valentines casino to do a photo shoot and have lunch. Why don't you all go get into the van and I will be right there," Sophia said.

"Are we going to meet Mr. Valentine?" Allison asked and then giggled.

"No. Mr. Valentine is out of town," Sophia answered.

"Victor can I speak with you for a moment," Sophia said and then waited for the girls to leave the room before she turned her attention to Victor.

"I called to see what information was found about our Raven, and so far nothing was found. I want you to keep a close watch on her and tell Crystal to find out what she can about her at lunch. Maybe she can find out something more," Sophia said.

"Okay, I will speak with her when we get to the casino," Victor said. Sophia and Victor kissed and then went out to the van.

Victor drove the van. The drive took about five minutes before they reached the sign that said 'Welcome to Valentines Casino'. After Victor parked and helped the girls out of the van. Crystal got out last.

"Crystal, I want you to find out all you can about Raven," Victor whispered into her ear as he helped her out of the back of the van. Crystal just nodded to him.

"Okay ladies, let's go in and do the photo shoot," Sophia said as she walked up to the front door of the casino. They were met by a man dressed as a bell hop.

"I am sorry, but we are not ready for the photo shoot. We are still setting up the area for you, why don't you have lunch?" said the bell hop.

"Okay ladies, there has been a change in plans. We are going to have lunch first. Why don't you do some gambling and I will come back and get you," Sophia said before leaving them.

Crystal and Megan went to a slot machine to play.

"Rave, so how do you like working for the Cowboy's Club so far?" Crystal asked as she put some money into the machine.

"I really like it, but I have to say this part of the job is more fun than being in the club," Megan said and then smiled.

"Yeah I know what you mean. What did you before you came here to Colorado?"

"I worked as an office manager for the Nashville towing company," Megan said remembering her undercover profile.

"What made you want to become a stripper?"

"I needed some excitement in my life and when I got here it was the only job that I could find," Megan tried to sound convincing with her answers.

"I see."

"I want to thank you again for letting me stay with you, Crystal. I have a question though, how was Sharron as a roommate?"

"She was ok at the beginning, but she turned out to be a real bitch when she got star dancer at the club. I was the star before her. I also danced here, in this casino before."

"Wow, did you meet Rocco Valentine?"

"Yes, I did a job for him a few days ago. It was a dancing job at a party."

"Mark asked me to be this month's star dancer," Megan said trying to see if she would get a reaction out of her.

"He did?" Crystal asked as she looked at Megan with an angry look in her eyes.

"Yes, he said that you could help me out."

"Yeah I will, look I have to go to the bathroom," Crystal said getting up from the slot machine that she was playing.

"Ladies, our table is ready, let's go eat," Sophia called to everyone.

Robert called JP after Mark left the Cowboy's Club and he was there alone.

"Hello JP, it is me," Robert said into the when JP answered the phone.

"Where are you?"

"I'm in the Cowboy's Club."

"Are you alone?"

"Yes, we have a week. Mark has left for Vegas."

"Did you look for cameras or any bugs?"

"I am looking now, but I think just to be on the safe side, we should get a crew in here to look."

"We will be right there. See you soon."

"Ok, see you then, bye," Robert said into the phone and then started looking around to see if there were any cameras in the club.

Robert went down into Mark's office in the basement to check for any cameras before going through any of the file cabinets and the computers. When he was satisfied that there were no security cameras he called JP back.

"Hey JP, it's me again. I think that we need to get a team in here to help me with the remodeling. Also, Victor is coming tomorrow to clean and restock the bar," Robert said into his cell phone.

"Okay, I will have a team come. We will be there soon. We will be dressed as a construction crew so that no one will be suspicious," Robert heard JP say in the phone.

Robert hung up and waited for them to arrive. In the meantime, he started to go through Mark's desk to see what he could find. Robert sat at the desk. It was a wood desk stained to look like a redwood. It had a glass top. He opened the top long, narrow drawer and found Mark's appointment book. He took the leather book and put it on top of the desk before he looked through the rest of the drawer. He found nothing but office supplies, pens and paper clips. He closed the drawer and opened the appointment book. He found appointments with clients and money amounts. He thought that was strange. He put the appointment book aside and started a pile for things to show JP when he got there. He then went through the rest of the desk and found a file drawer. Robert was going through the files when his cell phone rang. It was JP letting him know that he was outside. Robert went up to the bar area to let him in. JP was dressed in overalls and so were the other officers.

"What did you find so far?" JP asked, when Robert closed the door behind the crew.

"Not much, but what we need to do first is really act like we are remodeling this place. Have any of you done construction work?" Robert asked the officers.

Chapter 41

Victor waited until everyone went to their rooms before sneaking into Mark's bedroom and closing the door behind him. Victor noticed the big king size bed next to the window that over looked the swimming pool. The bed had a leather plush head board and on the ceiling above the bed was a mirror. He sat on the bed and looked up at his reflection in the mirror.

"That is fucking clever. I am going to get me one of these," he said as he got up from the bed and went on with his search of the room. He went over to the other side of the room and opened the sliding doors that looked like wooden window shades with slates that opened into the bathroom. He noticed the glassed in shower. He looked around the room, but there was nothing there that he was looking for. He went back into the bedroom and closed the sliding door behind him. He looked around on the wall for buttons or a fake wall that would lead to another room. Just then, the door opened and Sophia walked into the room.

"Did you find anything?" Sophia asked as she closed the door behind her.

"No, I am checking to see if he has a hidden room in here," Victor said as he continued to feel the walls, but found nothing.

Megan's call

Megan got up out of bed and used the bathroom. She thought it would be a good time to call Robert. When she got back into the bedroom, she called Robert on her cell phone. The phone rang and then she heard Robert's voice.

"Hello?" Robert said into the phone.

"Hi, I was calling to check in and let you know that I am here in Mark's house in Black Hawk," Megan whispered into the phone.

"I know. Mark told me that you were doing the car show in Black Hawk before he left. Don't worry I've been going over to the loft and checking on Katie," Robert said into the phone.

"I will call you when I am back in town," Megan said.

"Meg, we need you to see what you can find in the house. Is there any way that you can search the house for anything like client books or any clue to the murders?" Robert asked into the phone.

"I can try. I will call you back and let you know what I find," Megan said and then hung up.

She put on her shorts and tee shirt and grabbed her phone to use as a flashlight. She opened her bedroom door and walked into the sitting room. She went over to Crystal's door and listened to see if she was asleep. She then opened the door that led to the hall, and made her way to the stairs to the first floor of the house and to the library. She went down the stairs and listened to see if she could hear anyone before going into the living room. She didn't hear anything, so she went down the stairs to the first floor of the house. She didn't need to use the light on her phone because the light of the full moon shone through the windows and illuminated staircase for her. When she was at the bottom of the stairs, she went into the living room, and made her way down the hall to the library. As she got to the door, she listened to see if she could hear anyone inside. She very quietly opened the door and went into the dark room and closed the door behind her. Megan turned on the light on her phone and moved the light around the room to see what she could see. She decided that a good place to start looking was the desk. She went over to the desk and sat down in the chair and started her search. She opened the drawers in the desk and found some papers about the car show and some photos of the dancer's and little bios written up for publicity. Megan closed the drawer and shone her light around the room to look for a file cabinet. There was a four drawer cabinet in the corner of the room. She opened the drawers, but all she found were contracts of the dancers. She thought it was strange that the contracts would be here. She thought back to when JP told them that Sophia handled all of the interviewing and contracts. Why would they be here and not in her office at the club? Megan looked to see if she could find anything else. She saw Sharron Jenkins file but when she opened the folder it was empty. She put the folder back into the file cabinet and checked the other drawers, but found nothing of interest.

"I just need to lock this door before going downstairs in the basement," Sophia's voice could be heard at the door. Megan quickly turned off her light and then looked around the room for some place to hide. She found a closet in back of the room. She opened the door and went inside and carefully closed the door, trying not to make a sound.

She heard the door open and the light turned on in the library. She heard the voice of Sophia talking to someone.

"We are going to find the books and then we will have Mark right where we want him. When we get the client list, we will have him in our back pockets and then I will get what I deserve, the club and the money. Mark will be arrested and thrown into jail," Sophia said.

"Then we will own the club?" Victor asked.

"Yes, if it all works out as we planned and that little mishap we had didn't cause too many problems," Sophia said as she turned off the light and locked the door after closing it.

Megan slowly counted to fifty before she opened the closet door and walked out into the room. She walked to the door and listened before she opened it a little to see if anyone was out in the hall. When she heard no one there, she opened the door and went out into the hall, locking the door and then closing it behind her very quietly. Megan thought it be would best to go back to her room and call it a night before she got caught sneaking around the house.

"Hello, did you get the information that I asked you for?" Sophia asked into the phone.

"Yes I did, I am faxing the information to you now. I called the places that you asked me to and they didn't know and never heard of Nina Keller. We even checked with the State of Tennessee's City Hall they said that Nina Keller was born in Nashville, but they have no other records of her," a man's voice came over the phone.

"What did you find out about the other person?" Sophia asked, going to the library door and locking it, then going to the fax machine to get the papers on Nina Killer.

"Justin Peterson, I haven't found anything yet, but I am still looking into that for you."

"Okay thank you. Let me know when you find anything more, bye," Sophia said and then hung up the phone.

Sophia read the papers that were on the fax machine and found out that Nina Keller was not who she said she was. Sophia needed to find out who she was. Sophia decided that she would keep an eye on Nina…Raven…or whatever her name was. Sophia realized that it was time for Victor to go back to Denver and get all the files from her house and office at the club and bring them to Central City to her vacation house.

"What are all these amounts next to these names?" JP asked looking at Mark's appointment book.

"That is what we need to find out, there are names here from Washington D.C, New York, and these are really important people from the government," Robert said.

"Wait, this name is the owner of one of the biggest hotels in Las Vegas," JP said pointing to the name that was in the book.

"Mark is in Las Vegas now," Robert said.

"Detectives, we think we found something," an officer came into the office.

"What did you find?" JP asked following the officer into Sophia's office.

"Take a look at this file we found in the file cabinet," said a female officer sitting at Sophia's desk. JP and Robert looked at the file. It was a folder that had Sharron Jenkins name on the tab. In the folder was a contract dated a month before Crystal and Mark said that Sharron started dancing at the club.

"Look at this, she was on the payroll a month before she signed this," said the officer that was going through the computer.

"I am going to call Candy and have her check the date on the video of Sharron in the hotel room that we found in the safety deposit box," JP said leaving the office to make the call on his cell phone.

JP went back into Sophia's office to see what other clues Robert had found.

"I am having Candy find the date on the video," JP told Robert who was looking through Sophia's computer with a police officer.

"Great, when we get that information we can pinpoint when Sharron started working for the Cowboy's Club," Robert said.

"We need to know what is going on here with these names and amounts of money that is coming into the Cowboy's Club. Are they all investors, or is there something else going on here that we need to know about," Robert asked JP.

"Got me, your guess is as good as mine," JP said shrugging his shoulders. "After Candy calls me back, the Sergeant wants me to go and get the copy of the surveillance tape from the Sheraton and take a look at it and see if it will lead us to what happened to Seth Brooks," JP said.

"While you are doing that, I am going to run these names in this appointment book and find out what they have in common with the Cowboy's Club and Mark Willis. In the morning I am also going to see what Megan found at the house," Robert said.

It was 5:30 in the morning when Megan's alarm went off. She rolled over and hit the snooze button and then went back to sleep, it felt like she just closed her eyes before Crystal knocked on the door.

"Raven, are you getting up? It's time to get up and get ready for the car show," Crystal's voice came through the other side of the door.

"Yea, I am getting up," Megan yawned as she sat up in the bed and pulled the covers off, then put her feet onto the floor and stood up yawning and stretching.

"The schedule says there is going to be a yoga class down by the pool, then breakfast in the dining room, and after that we are going to do the photo shoot before the car show at 7:30," Crystal said as Megan came out of her room and into the sitting area where she found Crystal sitting on one of the chairs with a coffee cup in her hand looking at the schedule.

"You wouldn't happen to have one of those cups for me would you?" Megan asked sitting down in the chair beside Crystal's.

"Yes I do. It's over there on the desk by the television," Crystal said pointing to the television stand.

"We have a busy day ahead of us, we have a full day planned, and we are going to be at the car show all day, until 8 tonight. Then we need to do a promotional photo shoot for Valentines," Crystal said showing Megan the schedule when she sat down with her coffee. She glanced at it and then set the paper aside on the coffee table in front of their chairs.

They sat and drank their coffee before putting on their workout clothes, a pair of loose shorts and a tank top. When they were dressed, they went out for the morning yoga by the pool.

"Good morning ladies! I am Sue Lee and I am going to teach you yoga, but before we get started, let's center ourselves. Close your eyes and feel mother Earth beneath you. Feel the energy that is coming from her. Feel the grass between your toes caressing your bare feet. Now rock back onto your heels and now back to your toes, relax and let yourself go. Now when you come back to the center open your eyes," Sue Lee said. Megan opened her eyes and saw that Sue Lee was a small, Asian woman with short dark hair. She looked like dwarf standing with her hands cupped in front of her and legs spread, as she stood in front of the class.

"Do as I do, follow me," Sue Lee said.

Megan looked over at the patio and saw Sophia and Victor arguing about something. Sophia gave him a set of keys. Then she saw Victor storm back into the house. Sophia gave Megan a glare and then she walked back into the house.

"Miss, you need to follow me please. Keep your eyes up here, not over there," Sue Lee scolded Megan for not paying attention.

Megan brought her attention back to the instructor and followed through all the yoga poses.

"Good morning everyone, take a seat and we will have breakfast and go over what is going to happen today at the car show," Sophia said as she sat down at the head of the table. Megan and the others gathered around the table and sat down to eat their breakfast of eggs, bacon, toast, coffee and orange juice. Everyone ate and made small talk. After everyone was done eating Sophia told them the schedule of the day.

"First, we are going to take the van into Black Hawk to the car show. When we get there, I will show you where your booth will be and then the photographer will be around to take your photos with the car before the show starts. About a hundred photos of each of you will be printed out and given to you to autograph at the show. After, we are going to do some photos inside Valentines casino, Raven you are going to do some extra photos for your promotion. Are there any questions? If not, then you all better get ready. We will all meet at the van," Sophia said before getting up from the table and then leaving the room.

Megan looked over at Crystal who was staring at her with an angry look on her face.

Sophia met with Victor in the entry way next to the front door after everyone was upstairs in their rooms changing.

"Victor, I want you to take my car and go back to Denver and get all my files out of my office and then I want you to get all my files from my house. Bring them to my vacation house in Central City," Sophia said.

"Okay, I will call you when it is done," Victor replied.

Megan was coming down the stairs ready to leave when she overheard Sophia and Victor talking in the entryway room by the front door. Victor looked at her and wondered if she overheard their conversation.

"Raven are you ready to leave? I thought you were going to wait for Crystal," Sophia said when she saw her coming down the stairs.

"I just came down to leave. I'm sorry, did I interrupt anything?" Megan asked as she made believe that she didn't overhear them talking.

"No, I was just informing Victor that I was going to drive you all to the car show, that is all. Why don't you go and get in the van. I will be right out," Sophia said and then gave her a fake smile. Megan walked the rest of the way down the stairs and out the door.

"I wonder if she overheard what we were talking about?" Victor asked as he looked at Sophia with a worried look.

"If she did, we will have to take care of it, just in case I am going to keep my eye on her while we are here. When you get everything, call me," Sophia said and then left the house to go to the van.

"Hey Vic, are you going to be driving us to town?" Crystal asked coming down the stairs as Victor was about to leave the house.

"No, I have to go back to Denver and get some cleaning done for the construction crew," Victor said as he opened the door for her.

"Can you do me a favor? Will you grab the folder I forgot in Sophia's office and drop it off at my house in Denver?"

"Sure, but I need your key."

"No, just put it on the sun porch, or through the mail slot. Thanks I owe you one," Crystal said and then left to join the others in the van.

Chapter 42

Victor drove back to the Cowboy's Club and when he saw the construction trucks in the parking lot he was surprised. He got out of Sophia's car and knocked on the door and waited for someone to answer and let him in.

Robert came up the stairs from the office when he heard a knock on the door. He knew that Victor was going to come back to clean in back of the bar. He looked around and saw everyone was working before he went to let Victor in.

"Hello, you must be Victor, I am Justin," Robert said after he let Victor in and then closed the door behind him.

"Mark said that you would be here today, I am going to clean in back of the bar. I'm also going to get some files from Sophia's office," Victor said going to the bar to start his work.

"I would let you in her office, but we have a crew in there working and everything is a mess right now. You wouldn't even be able to find the file cabinet," Robert lied.

"Well, I need to get the files that she needs," Victor said as he stopped his work and looked at Robert.

"No one will be able to go in there until tomorrow morning. I am sorry. I can't allow anyone but the crew in there because we are not responsible or insured if you get hurt. If you tell me what files you need I can see if I can find them for you," Robert said shaking his head no.

"I will come back tomorrow morning then!" Victor said angrily and made his way back to the door.

"That will be fine I will let you go into the office, we will be done by then," Robert said going down the hall to Sophia's office relocking the door after Victor left the club.

"Raven, it's time for your break," Sophia said walking over to Megan's booth and putting a closed sign next to the car.

"Okay, thank you. I'm going to go take a nap in the van, I am not a morning person, it seems," Megan said as she walked to the van.

"I will come and wake you when it is time to go back to work," Sophia called to her.

Inside the Mirror

"Hello Robert, before you say anything, first let me apologize for the way I acted the last time we saw each other," Megan said into her cell phone. She hoped that he would forgive her so she could go on with her plan. There was a moment of silence on the phone, before he spoke
"What do you mean Megan?"

Megan took a deep breath before answering him, "Never mind, I have a question to ask you, will you meet me so we can talk?" she asked, hoping that he would agree to meeting with her.

"Where would you like to meet?" he replied, he needed to find out what brought her back and why she was following him.

"Will you meet me at the ghost town outside of Central City?"

"Sure, give me an hour and I will be there," Robert said then he hung up.

Megan thought to herself 'I need to make sure that he does not charm me like he has done in the past. The last time I fell in love with him and....'

Mirror

Sophia found Megan in the seat of the van sleeping. She watched her toss and turn like she was lost in a dream.

"Raven," Sophia said as she shook her.

She awoke rubbing her eyes and looked up at Sophia who was standing over her smiling.

"Is it time to go back to work?"

"Yes it is, but first you better redo your make up," Sophia said and then she helped Megan to her feet and they went back to the booth.

"Now that everyone has had their breaks, I am going to see about our lunches. If anyone asks, I will be back in a half an hour," Sophia said as she watched Megan fix her makeup.

"Okay, if anyone asks I'll let them know," Megan said fixing her eyeliner and mascara.

"So what did you find on the surveillance tapes of the parking garage? Ruth asked, going through the files and paperwork on her desk.

"Well Sarge, I found out that Seth Brooks was murdered and you will never believe who did it," JP answered going over to Ruth's desk and sitting down in the chair that was across the desk from her.

"Did you bring in the person that was responsible for the murder?" Ruth asked looking up at JP.

"No, I wanted to show you the tape before I arrested them," JP said handing Ruth a flash drive that held a copy of the surveillance tape.

"Well let's take a look," Ruth said as she inserted the flash drive into her computer and turned the monitor so that both she and JP could see it.

"So is this also going to tell us who left the envelope at the valet desk?" Ruth asked JP after she signed on to her computer.

"No, we are still looking into that," JP said.

Ruth clicked on the flash drive file and opened it to see what was on the drive. They watched as the video started. They could see Seth's rental car parked on the roof of the parking garage. They waited to see something happen and they didn't have to wait long. The video showed a white tow truck with the name Smith's towing painted in blue on the side of the truck, pull up into the space next to Seth's car. A man got out of the truck. He was wearing a pair of gray overalls, but you couldn't see the man's face in the video. The video showed him take a slim Jim out of the truck then walk over to Seth's car. He popped the lock on the driver's side door like a pro. When the car door was open, he went back to his truck and took out a cardboard box and brought it to the car and set it on the cement floor. The man opened the box and took out an oxygen tank, the big O2 was visible on the tape. He then turned the pressure valve on the oxygen and carefully placed oxygen tank under the driver's seat in the car, and closed the car door. He then absentmindedly looked up at the surveillance camera as he turned to retrieve the cardboard box.

Ruth gasped when she saw the face of the man, and then she paused the tape to get a better look at his face.

"That's Victor Marshall," Ruth said in a shocked tone to her voice.

"Yeah, it is, Sarge. This tape proves that he is our murderer."

They watched Victor get into his truck and drive away. They watched the car but nothing happened. They waited for something to happen on the tape. Next, they saw Seth Brooks coming towards the car holding a cigarette lighter in his hand. He opened the driver's-side door and got into the car, they could not believe what happened next. They were all glued to the computer monitor to see what would happen. She watched Seth light his cigarette, then before her eyes the car exploded in a ball of flame.

"I want you to go and pick up Victor Marshall and charge him for murder," Ruth said.

Sophia got out of the van and went into the house. She went into the library and called her back ground checker to see if they found any more information about Nina Keller.

"Hello, did you find any more information for me?" Sophia asked into the phone.

"I did find out that Nina Keller has no records in Tennessee, but I am still checking a few more leads in Colorado. I will call you back."

"Okay, well fax me what you have so far," Sophia said and then hung up.

JP arrived at Victor's house and knocked on the door. Victor came to the door and looked at JP standing on the porch accompanied by three uniformed police officers.

"Victor Marshall, you are under arrest for the murder of Seth Brooks," JP said as two of the officers put the handcuffs on Victor and brought him out onto the porch.

"Victor Marshall, you have the right to remain silent. Anything you say can and will be used against you in a court of law.

You have the right to consult an attorney before speaking to the police and to have an attorney present during questioning now or in the future.

If you cannot afford an attorney, one will be appointed for you before any questioning, if you wish.

If you decide to answer any questions now, without an attorney present, you will still have the right to stop answering at any time until you talk to an attorney.

Do you understand your rights as I have explained them to you?" JP asked while the officers escorted Victor to the police car.

Candy went into the interrogation room of the police station and waited for Victor Marshall to be brought in for questioning. Candy was going over the arrest file when Victor Marshall was escorted into the room by a police officer. Victor was in handcuffs and shackles and the officers pushed him down into the chair across from where Candy was sitting.

"Thank you, officer, please tell Detective John Paul to come in," Candy said looking at Victor who was sitting there looking down the floor.

"Good afternoon, Mr. Marshall, I am Detective Candice Carmon," Candy said introducing herself.

"Mr. Marshall, we will start in a moment, would you like to have your lawyer present during your questioning?" Candy asked.

"No, I think that I am going to pass on the lawyer for now," Victor replied looking at Candy.

"Well, that is up to you, but you are being charged of murder and we have the evidence of you doing the act. I would want a lawyer if I were you Mr. Marshall," Candy said looking at the arrest file.

"Hello Mr. Marshall," JP said entering the room and sitting down in the empty chair beside Candy's.

"I see that Detective John Paul and the arresting officer read you your rights during your arrest, so even now they apply. Do you understand your rights?" Candy asked looking at Victor who was sitting across the table and smiling.

"Yes I do, Detective Carmon," Victor replied in a macho tone. Candy just glared at the prisoner.

"So, I ask you again Mr. Marshall, would you like to have a lawyer present while I question you?" Candy said pushing the black phone over to the prisoner. Victor looked at the phone like it was going to give him the answer to a question before replying to Candy's question.

"No, I think I'll be okay, besides, you don't know the real murderer," Victor said and then smirked.

"Hello Mr. Marshall, I am Sergeant Ruth Toshibalua I will be sitting in during this questioning," Ruth said as she came into the interrogation room and took a seat.

"Sarge,you want to hear something funny? Victor here doesn't want a lawyer. He says we don't have any proof that he killed Seth Books," JP said smirking at Victor.

"We don't huh. Well it was your face on the surveillance tapes. Would you like to see?" Ruth said with an angry look on her face. Ruth got up from the chair and walked over to where Victor was sitting. She stood in back and leaned over his shoulder, and pulled over to him the folder that held the pictures from forensics of Seth's rental car. Victor looked at the pictures of the burned-out car, and then he looked away.

"That is what you did. Now, why don't we take a look at something else and then tell me if you think you don't need a lawyer," Ruth replied.

JP put his laptop on the table in front of Victor and then turned it on to view the video.

"Now you tell me what you see, Mr. Marshall, and explain what you're doing," JP said looking at Victor discussed. Victor watched the surveillance tape and could not believe that he had been caught in the act. After the scene that showed Victor getting back into his truck and leaving the parking garage, JP paused the tape.

"You know that was you Victor wasn't it?" JP said pointing his finger in Victor's face with anger. Victor just nodded his head in shame without speaking.

"Well, we got that clear. You admitted it was you, but what you don't know is the next scene. I am going to show you what happens," JP said looking at Victor to see if he would show any emotion. He un-paused the tape so that Victor could view the rest of the crime. Victor watched Seth get into the car, and then he watched as the car was engulfed in flames.

"Now, Mr. Marshall, I have to ask you again, would you like a lawyer during this questioning?" Ruth asked looking back at the man, then picking up the file off the table walking back to her chair to sit.

Ruth, Candy, and JP looked over at Victor who had a worried look on his face.

"I would like to call my lawyer, but you don't understand all of what happened. I didn't do it because I wanted to, but because I had to," Victor said looking at JP who was looking at him with interest.

"Go on, what do you mean 'you had to' Mr. Marshall? I would like to know what you have to say," Ruth said.

"I will tell you everything when my lawyer is here," Victor replied as he picked up the phone and dialed a number. Candy, JP, and Ruth left the room so that Victor could make his call.

"Hello, it's Victor I need help. I am at the Denver Police station," Victor said into the phone then pausing before speaking again.

"No, they don't know, but they have a surveillance tape from the garage and it shows me putting the oxygen tank into the car," Victor said with a worried tone in his voice.

"If you don't help me I will tell them it was you!" Victor shouted into the phone angrily.

"What do you mean that the lawyer is out of town until tomorrow? You mean I have to stay here until he gets back? Fuck you! I will! I will tell them everything....You better do something tonight," Victor screamed into the phone before slamming the receiver back down on the phone's cradle.

"So, did you get a hold of your lawyer?" Candy asked coming back into the questioning room and finding Victor smoking a cigarette and looking defeated like he just lost the big game.

"He is out of town. The law firm is trying to find someone that can come in his place," Victor said, looking at Candy, who was looking at him.

"Well, until then, we are going to have to put you down stairs in a holding cell," Candy said as she left the room.

"Do I get to make a call?" Victor asked the officer that escorted him to the holding cell.

"Yea you get one call, but you can make that call in the holding cell. You will have to call collect, but first, we need to book you," answered the officer who was bringing Victor to a metal chair. The officer waited for him to seat himself and the put the hand cuffs on his wrist and locked him to the metal bars on the chair.

"You wait here while I get the camera ready to take your mug shot and then we will do your finger prints," the officer said as he walked over to the camera in front of the mug shot area. He put the film in and got the fingerprint area set. He went back to un-cuff Victor so that he could take his mug shot and finger prints. When they were done, the officer put him into the holding cell and locked the door of the cell. Victor waited until the officer was down the hall before making his call.

Chapter 43

Robert was so tired from looking for evidence in the club that he took a nap on the sofa in Mark's office...

Inside the Mirror

Crystal stood and watched as Robert put his cell phone back into his pocket of his tight blue slacks. Robert looked at Crystal, knowing what her next lesson was going to be. Crystal had to go back to her life before she turned and that was not going to be easy. He had a difficult time with that lesson.

"Crystal now that you have eaten, I am going to bring you back home," Robert said then smiling at his new vampiress. Crystal looked back at him with confused look on her face.

"What do you mean Robert? What am I supposed to do?"

"You have to live the same as before," Robert said.

"Live, what do you mean? I don't know how to do that. Go back to work and live life, how do I do that?" Crystal asked. She began to cry as she thought about what her life was going to be like. Robert knew that it was going to be hard on her, but she had to do it and he would check in on her. He held her as she began to break down. He tried to comfort her and kissed her. He slowly went to the ground taking her with him as he passionately kissed her. He touched her and caressed her. Crystal melted into Robert's embrace and let him take her. He stood up and pulled her up with him and started to undress her as the two lovers began to float into the sky. The Cinderella gown fell and hit the ground. Crystal followed his lead and undressed him as well, until they were both in the sky flying naked. Robert's kiss got more sensual as he invaded Crystal's mouth with his tongue. He touched her naked body, getting her ready for him to take her. When he knew she was ready, he entered her. As he made love to her they floated higher and higher away from the ground up into the night sky. The Vampire and his Vampiress made love as the night air cooled their intertwined bodies. Crystal could feel Robert was going to finish, so she arched her back as he held on to her so she would not fall out of the sky. Robert bit on her out stretched neck. When the

lovers in the night sky were done Robert slowly released Crystal as she started to fall.

"My lover, be my night vampiress. Fly!" Robert called to his falling love. At that moment Crystal changed. She became the vampiress that she was made to become. She floated back up to Robert and they kissed in the night sky.

The air was cool. Megan could hear the sounds of leaves blowing in the wind. Her raven hair was blowing in the wind as she walked the dirt road looking at all the abandoned buildings. She felt the Earth beneath her feet. She closed her eyes and lifted her arms to the night sky, chanting and asking the Mother for strength to resist Robert's charms. She knew someone was watching her, she could feel him, his heart and soul. She could feel all of him. She felt for the stiletto dagger tucked under the sash of her long black gown. It was still there and waiting for her to use. She turned to face who was watching her in the shadows, her eyes searching while her mind knew who and where he was.

"Robert, I know you are here, I can feel you. Are you enjoying watching me? It has been a long time since I felt your heart beating. Yes Robert, I can still feel your heart," Megan said as she walked around the ghost town like she owned the place. She was waiting and watching for Robert to emerge from out of the dark shadows and show himself to her, but he didn't. Megan smiled then said, "My darling, I can wait all night if that is what it takes. I thought that we could bring back those old feelings again and see what happens," Megan cunningly cooed.

Robert watched and thought that Megan was acting too submissive toward him. She must have something planned. Robert looked at her body as she swayed by his hiding place and saw the glimpse of something shiny glistening in the light of the moon. At that moment he knew why she wanted to meet with him. She stopped walking and shook her head.

"I can feel you Robert, you are trying to get into my head and heart. I will let you if you show yourself. A man...I mean, a vampire, like you shouldn't be afraid of a woman like me. You used to love me at one

time...Robert... " *Before she could finish Robert quietly floated up to her, and wrapped his arms around her waist, so she could not grab the dagger hidden in the sash of her gown.*

"Megan, my love, that was long ago, before...I...Megan I know what is in your heart. I know there is love there for me still, but there is also hate, hurt, and revenge there," Robert whispered into her ear. That is when she turned to face the vampire that she come to love and hate through the lives that they shared. Robert looked into her eyes, he could see the love that she still had for him, he also loved her as well.

"Robert, we have been through so much together. Where do we go from here?" Megan asked with tears in her eyes, knowing what had to be done now. She kissed him as she pulled out the dagger and was ready to pierce it into his chest, when he suddenly pulled away from her kiss. He looked down at the dagger in the witch's hand.

"So is this what you had in mind, to kill me?" Robert growled as he pushed Megan to the ground. She got up and lunged for him. He blocked her blow with his fist. He hit her in the face and knocked her back. Megan could feel and taste the blood from her lip where his fist made contact with her face. She spat out the blood and lunged for him again, this time holding the dagger above her head, ready to stab her target. She knew she could wound him if necessary, so she would have the chance to pierce his heart later. As she lunged at him, Robert put his arm up to block her blow and the dagger caught him in the shoulder. He could feel the warm blood flowing from his shoulder, but that didn't stop him from pushing Megan away.

Crystal was hiding in the shadows watching the fight between Megan and Robert. She saw the blood flowing from Robert's shoulder and knew she had to help him. Crystal ran up behind Megan. Megan didn't realize she was there until it was too late. Crystal grabbed Megan from behind and started hitting her. Megan tried to fight her off, grabbing at her, but Crystal had her arm around Megan's neck and was ready to bite her. Robert looked over at the two women fighting and saw that Crystal was about to sink her fangs into Megan's neck.

"Crystal, NO! You must not bite her!" Robert yelled and lunged for the two women, hitting Crystal and knocking her to the ground. The dagger fell to the ground in the struggle and Megan grabbed for it. She

lunged for Crystal who lay on the ground on her back. Robert grabbed Megan by the arm and knocked the dagger from her grasp before it made contact with Crystal's chest. Megan dove for the dagger as it hit the ground, but missed it when Robert kicked it away from her grasp.

"Megan, please don't do this," Robert said tenderly. Megan looked up at him standing over her.

"Robert, I have to put a stop to all of this before it gets out of hand. I am sorry but I have to do this," Megan said as she grabbed for the dagger and made a lunge for the vampiress who was now getting to her feet once again. Megan pushed the vampiress to the ground and Megan sat on top of her holding her down on the ground. She plunged the dagger into Crystal's chest. Robert watched as the fight ended. Crystal screamed and tried to pull out the dagger all the while trying to bite at Megan. Robert punched Megan, knocking her to the ground, then, ignoring the burning pain, pulled the dagger out of Crystal's chest and held her head in his arms. She looked up at him with pain and love in her eyes.

"Robert my love, am I going to die again?" She asked as tears rolled down her face. He looked down at his vampiress and saw that blood was gushing out of the wound that the dagger made in her chest. Then he forced a smile to come to his face, looking back into Crystal's face.

"You will be ok, I am here with you my love, and I am going to make it easier for you. Do you trust me Crystal?" Robert asked as he took up the dagger. The dagger burned in his hand with pain he had never known before. He stifled a cry as he plunged the blade deep into Crystal's heart and twisted it until he knew she was dead. Megan watched as Robert pushed the dagger farther into Crystal. Megan knew that she had to get the dagger back so she could finish her task. Robert looked up at Megan glaring and baring his fangs, all the while knowing that he could not bite her, but he wanted to. Robert released the dagger and held Crystal in his arms, as she aged before his eyes. She let out one last breath and her body disintegrated into ash in his arms. The dagger fell to the ground in the ash. He picked it up, grimaced in pain and pointed the dagger at Megan who was lunging to grab it.

"What would happen if I use this on you now?" Robert growled at Megan with revenge in his eyes. Megan grabbed at the dagger, but Robert pushed her away forcefully, and she fell back onto the ground. As

she fell, she banged her head on a rock, knocking herself out. Robert looked at her body lying on the ground then he looked at the rock where she banged her head, it was stained red with her blood....

Mirror

Robert awoke to the ringing of his cell phone, but when he answered the phone, it was too late, the call went to his voice mail. He listened to the message.

"Robert it's Megan...I am calling to let you know that I am going to search the house again...I will call you when I get back to my room," Megan's voice said into the phone.

Robert tried to call Megan, but all he got was her voice mail.

"Detective, I think we found something. There is a hidden safe in Sophia's office. We are trying to open it, now," said a police officer as he came into Mark's office to find Robert sitting on the sofa.

"Maybe we will find something in there, so far we haven't found anything," Robert said with a spark of hope as he got up and followed the officer back to Sophia's office.

It was around two in the morning when Megan left her room to go down stairs look for clues in the house. She decided to go down into the wine cellar to see what she could find. She checked to make sure everyone was in their rooms for the night before going down the stairs to the first floor. Megan went to the back of the house and found the door that led down to the wine cellar. She opened the door, turned on the light and descended the carpeted stairs. In the wine cellar was a bar area and sitting room. Megan walked around the sitting room found a door in the back of the room. She tried to open it, but it was locked. Megan moved into the bar area, it was filled with shelves of wine bottles and nothing out of the ordinary. Megan wondered what could be behind the door in the sitting room that was so important that Mark kept the door locked. She decided that the key to the room could be in the library, so she went back up to the library to see if she could find the key.

Crystal awoke to the sound of her phone ringing. She sat up in her bed and answered the cell phone before the sound of the ringing woke Nina up.

"Hello?" Crystal said answering the cell phone on the night stand beside her bed.

"Hello Crystal, this is Mark," Mark's voice came over the phone.

"Hi Mark what do you need?"

"I need you to listen really close and do what I say. Is Sophia still there?"

"Yes, she is here, but she is sleeping in her room. Why? Do you want me to go get her?"

"No, I need for you to do something for me. Don't tell anyone that I called you and asked you to do this. Go down stairs into the library. In back of the Picasso painting is a safe. The combination to the safe is 33-66-99. In the safe there is a key ring. Take the key ring, and go down to the basement. Find the office. It is the only door that is locked. There are five file cabinets in there. Look for the file drawer marked with the red smiley face. Open it and you will find a briefcase in there, it's hidden behind some files. I need you to take the briefcase and hide it for me at your house until I return from Vegas," Mark instructed then he hung up the phone. Crystal slipped on her shorts and left her bedroom to do what Mark asked of her.

Megan went into the library to look through the desk. When she didn't find the key she decided to look through the file cabinet. Megan was going through the file cabinet when she heard the door knob to the library turn like someone was opening the door to come in, before she could do anything she was hit in the head and fell to the carpeted floor, unconscious.

Victor slammed the phone down in anger, almost pulling the phone off the cell wall.

"What's wrong? Did you get the wrong answer?" laughed the guard as he walked by the holding cell.

"I would like to talk to the officer that arrested me," Victor said with anger in his voice as he turned and faced the guard.

"You will have to wait until morning, but you could speak with me," the guard laughed again as he walked away.

"Come back!" Victor yelled angrily hitting the bars of the cell.

"Lights out!" the guard yelled and then shut off the lights leaving the prisoners in the dark. It was not long before the lights came back on again and the guard went to Victor's cell.

"Go to the wall and face the wall with your hands up above your head," the guard instructed. Victor did as he was told, before the gaurd opened the door and put the handcuffs on Victor. The guard escorted him from the cell to the interrogation room and cuffed him to a metal chair. JP came into the room and sat down in the chair opposite to Victor. The two were separated by a long metal table.

"I need to ask you a question Victor," JP said.

"Okay, what do you want? First, can I get a cigarette from you?" Victor asked.

"I don't smoke" JP said, and then he thought that he would get more information he needed if he got the man what he wanted. "Wait here. I will see what I can do," JP said leaving the room.

"Where am I gonna go," said Victor with a sneer.

It didn't take long before JP was back holding a full pack of cigarettes in his hand.

"I will give you these if you will give me the information that I need," JP said holding out the pack of cigarettes to Victor, taunting him with them.

"Sure whatever," Victor said reaching for the pack.

"I need the combination to a safe that we found in Sophia's office at the Cowboy's Club," JP said hoping that Victor knew the safe combination so they could open it.

"The combination? I don't know it, but I can find out if you let me use my cell phone and call Sophia. I am supposed to be at the club getting something for her anyway," Victor said.

JP thought about it for a moment then he agreed to let Victor make the call and left the cigarettes on the table for Victor while he went to get the cell phone. The guard came into the room and lit a cigarette for

Victor with a lighter. Victor smoked the cigarette enjoying each drag. JP came back and put the cell phone onto the table before sitting back down in his chair. Victor picked up the cell phone and dialed Sophia's number, but there was no answer. The call went to Sophia's voice mail. He left a message for her.

"Sophia, this is Victor, call me back as soon as possible," he said into the phone then he hung up. JP decided that they should wait for Sophia to call back.

"Victor, why did you kill Seth Brooks?" JP asked with a curious look on his face.

"I can't say why, but if I had to do it over again, I would have done it differently," Victor said.

"And how would you do it differently?"

"Well for one, I wouldn't have gotten caught."

"Did you kill Sharron Jenkins?"

"I think I explained that I had an alibi for that one and you cleared me of that. I am done talking. If you want any more information after I get the call from Sophia, I want my lawyer present," Victor said angrily slamming his fist on the table. JP shook his head and got up and left the room. After he left, the guard came into the room and sat down with his newspaper.

Robert went right into Ruth's office when he got back to the police station. Ruth looked at him with surprise on her face. Why would he be so bold as to come into her office without knocking on the door first?

"Detective, what can I do for you?"

"Sergeant, I found proof that the Cowboy's Club is a cover for prostitution. We found out that Sharron Jenkins was on the payroll even before she made out the application to work there."

"What do you mean? Explain yourself Detective."

"Okay, look at this appointment book that I found in Mark's office at the Cowboy's Club. Here, it shows his investors and also his clients. This shows how much they paid him and these are the amounts that the dancers got paid according to the spread sheets we found on Sophia's computer. These are the payments clients paid the dancers, but you can see here that the same amount is not in the paystubs of the dancers,"

Robert explained showing Ruth the spreadsheets, paystubs, and the payroll documents from the Denver Bank. Ruth examined all the documents and found that none of them added up with the amounts that the clients and investors paid out and the Cowboy's club took in.

"It looks like here on Sharron's payroll that she got paid this amount from the club. Then it shows here the client paid more for an extra three hours on this day. It shows that the club added extra money and paid for a room at this hotle for the night on the same day. It shows money going out of the club and payroll. It doesn't show on the spread sheet or the paystubs that Sharron got paid overtime, maybe she got paid in cash," Ruth said as Robert looked at the documents.

"What do we do now?" Robert asked wondering how they could prove what they found.

"Where is Mark Willis now?"

"He is in Las Vegas, but I don't know where he is staying."

"Okay, I will find that out from Victor Marshall."

Chapter 45

The day after Crystal got back from Black Hawk, she called in a missing person report to the Denver Police Department.

"Hello, I am calling because my roommate Nina Keller is missing," Crystal said into the phone to the police officer who answered the call.

"How long has she been missing?"

"She went missing the day before yesterday," Crystal answered.

"Where was the last place you saw Miss Keller?" the officer asked.

"We were in 555 Highway 73 in Golden," Crystal lied.

"We will start looking for her, but if you hear from her or she comes home let us know."

"I will, thank you," Crystal said and then hung up the phone.

Crystal thought she should call Mark and let him know that she was home and that she had the briefcase with her.

When Megan awoke she found herself tied up on a bed. The room was dark, except for the moonlight shining through a window. She looked around. It looked like she was in a cement cellar. She tried to get up off the bed but the straps around her body held her down. She couldn't move. Megan felt anxiety build up, but she thought that she needed to calm down and think with a clear mind on what she needed to do. She wondered where she could be. The last thing that she remembered she was in the library at Mark Willis's house. She was looking for a key and then she heard someone coming into the room and then she was hit in the head.

Robert called Megan's cell phone to see if she was back from the car show.

"Hello, you have reached Megan Sapphire. I am not able to answer your call. Leave a message and I will call you back," said Megan's voicemail. Robert didn't leave a message.

He figured that he would call her back later, and wondered why she was not answering her phone. He couldn't keep his eyes open so he laid down and went to sleep...

Inside the Mirror

Robert's cell phone rang...
"Hello," Robert said into the phone.
"Hi, Robert it is Sharron, have you seen or heard from Crystal?"
Sharron asked, she sounded worried.
"Oh, Sharron, she is at my ranch. I was just going there now. She just told me this morning that she wanted to see you."
"Wow, it's good to hear that she is alright. I have been worried. It has been over a week since I saw her or talked with her," Sharron said with a sigh of relief.
"Well, I am headed into town right now. I could pick you up and bring you back home this evening," Robert said, trying to convince Sharron into trusting him.
"That sounds great. I will meet you in front of the Clock Tower this afternoon at twelve," Sharron said.

It was twelve in the afternoon when Robert picked Sharron up on the side of the road in front of the Clock Tower.
"I was hoping that Crystal would be with you," Sharron said as she got into the car.
"She is at the ranch, making lunch for us," Robert said with a smile as he drove down the street headed out of town toward the ranch.

"What happened to you, miss?" Asked a blonde woman who was wearing a ranger's uniform. When Megan awoke she found herself in a room on a cot.
"What is your name?" the ranger asked.
"What happened...? Ouch, my head hurts," Megan said, as she put her hand up to her head and felt the bandages.
"What were you doing out in the ghost town all alone?" the Ranger asked tending to Megan's cut lip.
"I was.... what do you mean...where am I...who am I?" Megan looked around with a strange unknowing look on her face.

Robert took Sharron into the house.

"Would you like something to drink?" Robert asked as he escorted Sharron to the sofa that was in front of the kitchen.

"Yeah, a glass of red wine, where is Crystal?" Sharron asked as she made herself comfortable on the sofa. Robert went into the kitchen to get her a glass of wine. She was looking out the window at the horses galloping in the pasture. She didn't notice Robert sneaking up behind her with his fangs bared until it was too late. The pigs ate well that night.

Mirror

Robert awoke to find Ruth standing next to the sofa.

"Robert we just got a call from the missing persons department, it seems that Crystal Stone called in a missing report on a Nina Keller this morning. I am waiting for Candy to bring her in so we can question her about the report," Ruth said sitting down next to him on the sofa in the police lounge.

"What do you mean? Megan is missing?" Robert asked with worried look on his face and worry in his voice.

"Yes, Crystal said that she has been missing for two days now. You haven't talked with Megan have you?"

"No Ruth. I just called her cell and got her voice mail."

"I want you to go with JP while we are questioning Crystal Stone. He is getting a search warrant to check Crystal's house for Megan," Ruth said

"If anything happens to Megan I…"

"We will find her," Ruth said trying to comfort Robert.

The room was pitch black and Megan couldn't see a thing. She struggled against the straps, but couldn't move. She heard the door to the room that she was in creak open and then the heavy door slammed shut and the click of the lock. She heard a click as the straps that held her down unhooked and allowed her to get up from the bed. The lights turned on and she could see the room. No one was there. The room consisted of a bed, a round wooden table with a basket of fresh fruit, and a wooden chair seated at the table, in the corner was a toilet. The walls were cement. There was only a small window that not even Katie could fit through. Megan took a deep breath and decided that she should eat and think about how to escape from this prison that she found herself in.

    Crystal Stone walked into the interrogation room and sat in the seat next to the desk and waited for Candy to come in to question her.

    "Hello Miss Stone how are you doing today?" Candy asked, coming into the room and sitting at the desk.

    "Hello Detective Carmon," Crystal replied.

    "The reason I asked you to come in is because I want to ask you some questions about your new roommate and her disappearance. This is the second roommate that has gone missing. We are trying to find out if you could be involved with Miss Jenkins and now Miss Keller's disappearances. It just seems strange to me that you have two roommates and they both go missing. Just to let you know, we have a team searching your house now."

    "What do you mean searching my house? I will sue you and the police department," Crystal said as she got up to leave.

    "Miss Stone, I think you had better wait here until we are done. I have a search warrant to search your house and also I am going to detain you until the search is complete, or we find your roommate," Ruth said coming into the interrogation room and blocking the door so that Crystal could not leave the room. Crystal sat back down in the chair.

    "Now Miss Stone, tell me the last time you saw your roommate," Candy asked.

    "The day before we left Mark Willis' house in Black Hawk, we were promoting the club at the car show," Crystal said nervously. Ruth and Candy noticed the nervousness in Crystal's tone and the way she rubbed her hands together.

    "In the report you said the last place you saw her was 555 Highway 73 in Golden. Which was it? There or in Black Hawk?"

    "Nina went to Golden after the show."

"With who?"
"I don't know. Someone she met at the car show."
"You don't know their name, but you know their address?"
"I don't want to say anymore."

Megan sat at the table and ate an apple out of the fruit basket.

"Who would have kidnapped me? And why was I taken? What do they want?" Megan asked herself.

As she looked around the room and tried to come up a plan of how she was going to escape the room. Just then she heard footsteps from the floor above her.

"Hello! I am down here!" She yelled to the owner of the feet above her hoping that it was someone that could help her…

"What are we going to find when we search your house?" Candy asked Crystal, who was moving around in the chair she was sitting in.

"Nothing, you are going to find nothing," Crystal said angrily.

Just then Candy's cell phone rang, she answered the call.

"Hello?" Candy said.

"We are at Crystal Stone's and we've found something. We are coming into the station, hold Crystal there," Robert's voice said into the phone then hung up before Candy could find out what they found.

Sophia drove up the driveway to her house in Central City. She got out of the van and took the groceries out of the back and walked to the front porch of a log two-story house. After putting the food away, Sophia went into her home office and turned on her computer. She went through the folders and found the Cowboy's Club investors. She found the name of one that sparked her interest. The name was Rocco Valentine.

She picked up the phone to call to Rocco but hung up the receiver before he could answer the phone. Sophia got up and went to the bar in the corner of the room and poured herself a brandy to calm her nerves.

Just then, the phone rang. She went over to the phone, took a deep breath and answered the call.

"Hello?" she said, hoping that it was Victor calling to let her know that he was on his way. She wished that before she left Mark's house that she had grabbed her cell phone, but she was in a hurry.

"We need to talk. Meet me at the club!" Mark angrily yelled into the phone before hanging up.

Sophia made a call and then left the office after hanging up the phone.

"Now, I need to finish what I started," Sophia said to herself angrily. She snatched her keys off of the desk and left the office.

Chapter 46

Victor looked over at the guard sitting in the chair, reading his newspaper and reached for the pack of cigarettes on the table.

"Can I have a light?" Victor asked, taking out a cigarette from the pack and putting it in his mouth. The guard lit the cigarette for him and then he took one for himself and lit it.

"Can I try my call again?" Victor asked.

"Sure," the guard said giving him the cell phone.

After Victor made his call and got Sophia's voice mail once again, it made him mad and he thought that maybe he should call her house phone.

"Can I try one more number?"

"Sure."

Victor called Sophia's home phone, but all the phone did was ring without anyone answering. After about ten rings, he hung up the phone and finished smoking his cigarette.

"I need to talk to that Detective John Paul or your Sergeant," Victor said out of the blue.

The guard opened the door and called for an officer.

"Jackson get me Detective JP or Candy!" and then closing the door.

Faith was sitting at the front desk when JP and Robert walked through the front door of the police station.

"Detectives, Victor Marshall is ready to talk to you," Faith said looking up at them.

"Okay, Faith, will you give this to Sergeant Toshibalua, and tell her that it's all we found at Miss Stone's house..." Just then JP's cell phone rang and he answered the phone.

"Hello...Are you sure... you heard something down there...how many rooms are down there...go through them and if they are locked break them down if you have to...call me when you find something," JP said into his phone then hung up.

"What is going on?" Robert asked, wondering what the crew heard.

"The crew thinks they heard something moving around in the basement. They will call me if they find anything. Now let's find out what Mr. Marshall wants to talk to us about," JP said walking towards the holding cells to the interrogation room that held Victor.

JP was about to open the door to the room when Robert stopped him.

"I think I better go into the viewing room, because Victor still knows me as Justin Peterson," Robert said.

"Yeah, you are right, and if he is going to confess to everything, he doesn't need to know that you are working with us," JP said, agreeing with Robert, and going into the room alone.

"Okay, I'm back. I was told that you wanted to speak with me Mr. Marshall," JP said when he came into the integration room.

Robert went into the viewing room and turned on the speakers so he could hear what was being said in the integration room.

"Okay, before we start, I am going to have Officer Winters record what you have to say," JP said.

"Okay," Victor said as he watched Officer Winters turn on the camera that was resting on the table.

"Okay, you can start when you are ready. We need you to state that you have been read your Miranda rights and that you are deciding to say this without a lawyer present," JP said before Victor started to speak his mind.

"I am Victor Marshall. I have been read my rights and I am giving my confession without my lawyer as I requested," Victor said as he picked up a cigarette and Officer Winters tossed JP his lighter so he could light Victor's cigarette for him. JP lit Victor's cigarette and then put the lighter on top of the pack of cigarettes.

"I killed Seth Brooks. You have proof on the surveillance tape from the parking garage, but I didn't want to do it. I was paid to do it," Victor replied taking a drag off his cigarette.

"Who paid you to kill Mr. Brooks?" JP asked wondering who wanted Seth dead.

"She was the one that left the envelope on the valet desk," Victor answered, thinking if he should just blurt out her name without explaining why she wanted Seth dead. He decided that he should explain why they killed Seth; maybe it would lessen his shame and guilt.

"Who is she?" JP asked.

"Before I tell you that, we need to go back to the beginning. Before I worked as a bartender at the club, I was doing private work for Mark Willis and his investors. That was the first time that I met Sharron Jenkins. She was working for Mark, but not in the club," Victor said taking another drag off of the cigarette that he was holding between his thumb and ring finger, like he was smoking a joint.

"If she wasn't working at the club, what was she doing?" JP asked wondering if they were right with their assumptions.

"Mark has many roles for his new applicants. Let's just say.... that he pays for rooms and penthouses at hotels and calls them business expenses and files his taxes that way. Sharron was a naive country girl, at least that's the role she played," Victor said shaking his head thinking back to the first time that he and Sharron met....

"Victor, this is Sharron Jenkins, I want you to be nice to her and show her what she needs to learn," Mark said when he escorted her into the room where Victor was waiting. Mark sat down on the sofa to watch the show with another man wearing a business suit. Victor remembered walking over to Sharron and kissing her. Out of the corner of his eye, he saw the man give Mark a rolled up wad of money. Mark took the money and put it in his jacket pocket.

Victor remembered that Sharron danced around the room and stripped, then she went to Victor and took off his clothes, she pushed him onto the bed and rubbed her body on him as she watched the man that was sitting in the chair hand Mark more money and whisper something into Mark's ear.

"Vic, grab your clothes, we're leaving," Mark said and then they left the room. Sharron was left with the client.

"Sharron was a prostitute and Mark started being her pimp. She was a fucking slut," Victor said referring to Sharron Jenkins. JP waited for Victor to go on with his story.

"Mark found out that one of his sluts was keeping money from him, so he made Sharron go on a job with her. Mark told me to get the money, and do what I had to do to get it from her. So I slapped the bitch around and I fucked her until she gave me the money. I am not proud of the shit I did, but, hell, I was getting paid a lot of money to do it. Mark decided that he was going to remodel the club and he needed some hot new dancers. That is when Sharron got the job as barmaid. Then she wanted to be a dancer. She found out about Mark's plans and she told us that she had an ex that was an architect and that he would remodel the club. After a while, we found out that Sharron and Seth were going to blackmail Mark for prostitution. We were pissed, cuz that was our fucking plan!" Victor said.

What do you mean 'we'?" asked JP.

"I'm getting to that. The woman I was working with, me and her had a plan to get the files from Mark and get him to pay up or we would ruin his business. He had a lot of dangerous guys as clients and they wouldn't want this to get out. So, we figured he would pay big. But, damn Seth and Sharron were going blackmail the fucker, too. We had to put a stop to that. So I played as Sharron's lover and that was when I told my partner that we needed to keep Sharron where we could keep an eye on her, that is when we found a place for her to live," Victor said trying to explain what happened.

"So that is when she moved into Crystal Stone's house?" JP asked, wondering if Crystal was his partner, but before he could ask Victor started back telling his story.

"Yeah, she moved in with Crystal. There we could watch her every move. The morning that Sharron went missing, we kidnapped her and took her out of town. Then, her body was found in the park. I didn't kill Sharron. All I did was kidnap her."

"After Sharron was dead, we thought that her and Seth's plan was put to an end, but Seth was still going on with the plan. So my partner said that we had to take care of that problem too. She told me how she wanted it done. So we got the oxygen tank and I rented the tow truck, then I.... well you saw what I did on the tape. Now that we had problem number two taken care of, that is when Justin and that new dancer Raven came into the picture," Victor said, putting out his cigarette in the ashtray on the table in front of him. When JP heard the undercover names of Robert and Megan he sat up in his chair and leaned over the table closer to hear what Victor had to say.

"While we were in Black Hawk, at Mark's house, we were looking for files of Mark's clients so we could blackmail them into giving us money and leaving Mark out of the deal. My partner had Raven, I believe her real name is Nina something, checked out and had someone do a background check on her. We also had that Justin Peterson guy checked out, but before I could find out anything on them, that is when my partner said that there was something wrong with their backgrounds. She sent me back to Denver and told me to go the club and grab some files and bring them to her house. Then I was arrested," Victor said lighting another cigarette and taking a drag "And that's it."

JP thought about what they found at Crystal's house in the briefcase.

"I have to ask you again who your partner is. Is it Crystal Stone?" JP asked Victor, who had a surprised look on his face.

Megan sat back on the bed then she heard a voice come over the intercom in the ceiling. The voice sounded like it was disguised with some kind of voice changing software.

"I know who you are, Megan Sapphire. You are a private Detective. You used to work for the Denver Police Department for years before you left and started your own private Detective agency with Robert Towers, who is posing as Justin Peterson," the voice said over the intercom.

"Who are you? And where am I?" Megan yelled at the ceiling.

Robert left the viewing room and ran up the stairs to the interrogation room where Candy and Ruth were questioning Crystal Stone. When he got to the room, he found it empty. Robert then closed the door and went into Ruth's office without bothering to knock on the door. Ruth looked up at him when he barged in.

"You know Detective Towers, this is getting on my nerves. You busting into my office without knocking," Ruth said.

"Where's Crystal?" Robert asked wondering why she was not in the questioning room.

"We let her go home, the team called and the Captain said that they didn't find anything at the house. He told us that we could not detain her any longer."

"Was that before or after the team called JP about the sound they heard in the basement?" Robert asked worriedly.

"What basement? and what sound?," Ruth said getting on the phone and calling the Captain to find out the answer, while Robert went and found Candy to get Crystal's address...

Megan heard the intercom turn back on.

"I am going to bring you some dinner. I want you to lay on the bed put your arms next to your body and put your legs flat on the bed," the voice instructed Megan. She lay down on the bed and did as she was told and the straps fastened around her legs and her wrists trapping her on the bed so she could not move. It wasn't long before she could hear the door to her room unlock and footsteps walking over to the table behind the headboard of the bed.

"Who are you and why did you kidnap me?" Megan asked her capturer, but there was no answer, just silence. She heard the plate cling on top of the wooden table and a glass placed on the table. Megan sniffed the air in hopes that she could smell some scent of her capturer, but she couldn't smell anything, just meatloaf and gravy. She heard the door close and lock. She waited until the straps where released before she got out of the bed.

"Megan, enjoy this meal because this may be the last one you'll get before I kill you," the voice said. Megan looked at the plate of mash potatoes, carrots, meatloaf, and biscuit smothered in brown gravy and at the glass of milk on the table.

"Should I eat this?" Megan asked herself out loud.

"Be assured that I would not bother killing you without you seeing me do it. You are safe to eat your food, Detective. I promise I didn't poison it," the voice answered. Megan could hear her stomach growling. She was fighting between her mind telling her not to trust the food, and her stomach that could smell the food. The fight went on briefly until her stomach won the fight, and she sat down at the table to eat.

"So, how long do you plan on keeping me locked up here?" Megan asked.

"Oh I don't know. I may just let you starve here while I am in Las Vegas. Or maybe I'll find your partner and have him keep you company, or kill you both and then sell the house."

Then all went quiet.

"I hope you enjoyed you dinner, now I want you to go back on the bed," the voice said when she was done eating. Megan thought that her kidnapper must be able to see her as well as hear her. Megan did as she was told. When she went to lie down she put her arm under her leg and noticed that the straps did not lock completely. The straps looked like they were locked into place to the side of the bed. Then she heard the door open and someone walked into the room.

"Do I know who you are? Have I met you before?" Megan asked her capturer...

Robert ran back down stairs and busted his way into the interrogation room.

When Victor saw him, his face went white and then he asked "What the fuck are you doing here, Justin?"

"I am not Justin. I am Detective Robert Towers and I need to ask you some questions," Robert said looking at Victor.

"What do you want to know? I thought you were a contractor?" Victor said sarcastically.

Robert pulled Victor out of the chair and pushed him up against the wall.

"Look, you son of a bitch, I want you to tell me who your partner is or I will beat you until you do," Robert yelled into Victor's face.

"If you do I will sue you and the whole Denver Police Department for police brutality."

"Go ahead, your case won't hold up in court because I am not on the police force. Hell, I don't work for them, but your partner has my partner and I want to know who that is," Robert said slapping Victor in the face with his open hand.

"Is it Crystal Stone?" JP asked again.

"Maybe, I won't tell you now! I want my fucking lawyer!" Victor screamed.

"I am your fucking lawyer now, fucker!" Robert yelled and started to punch Victor in the face and he punched him again and didn't stop until JP stepped in.

"Robert if you kill him, we won't find out where Megan is and who has her."

Megan held her arms like they were strapped to the bed.

And she asked again, "Do I know you?"

The kidnapper held a stiletto dagger, which is a thin blade with a sharp point at the end used in the medieval days for assassinations. Megan's capturer held the ivory handle in her hand behind her back ready to use it.

"Yes, you know me. We have met before," her capturer said.

It was Sophia. Megan didn't understand why Sophia had done it.

"Megan, I will not let you or anyone stand in my way of getting what is mine," Sophia said lunging at Megan with a look of hate in her eyes. Megan still acting like she was strapped to the bed just watched, until the dagger came towards the side of her neck. Without knowing that Megan's arms were not locked into the straps on the bed, Sophia tried to stab her in the side of the neck with the tip of the blade, Megan grabbed Sophia's hand as she sprung up from the bed and the two women struggled with the knife. Sophia pushed Megan back onto the bed and again tried to stab her with the dagger. Megan rolled Sophia off of her and got on top and punched Sophia in the face. Sophia pushed Megan off of her onto the floor and lunged for her again with the dagger. Megan grabbed Sophia's hand and slammed it onto the floor until she dropped the dagger. Megan pushed Sophia onto the floor and put her pulled her wrist behind her back.

Just then, Megan heard the sound of someone coming down the stairs. 'Oh shit, another one' she thought. Sophia twisted away from Megan and Megan fell to the floor. She hit the floor head first and was knocked out.

Sophia looked at Megan and saw that she was not moving. 'Time to die, bitch!" she said. She lunged at helpless body lying on the floor. As Sophia was about to plunge the blade into Megan's chest, she felt a strong hand grab her arm and pull her off the helpless woman.

"Sophia Abbott, you are under arrest for the murder of Sharron Jenkins and the attempted murder of Detective Megan Sapphire. You have the right to remain silent. Anything you say can and will be used against you in a court of law. You have the right to have an attorney present, if you do not have one, one will be appointed to you. Do you understand these rights I have just read to you?" JP said as he took Sophia's arm from Robert's grasp and put the handcuffs around her wrists.

Robert went to check on Megan. She was not moving. When he put his hand under her head he felt the warm liquid of her blood oozing from her head.

Sophia sat in the interrogation room waiting for her lawyer. She was furiously rocking back and forth in her chair, shaking her head. The door opened and JP and Candy walked in and sat down in the chairs across from where she was sitting.

"Miss Abbott, I am going to ask you some questions," Candy said glaring at Sophia.

"I want my lawyer," Sophia said without looking at Candy.

"Miss Abbott, your lawyer is not coming, but we will get one for you," JP said.

Sophia thought about what she could do to get herself out of the charges she was facing. She came to the opinion that she had to cooperate with them.

"None of this would have happened if Mark would have given us our half of the profits," Sophia said angrily.

"What do you mean half of your profits?" JP asked.

"My ex-husband is an investor in the Cowboy's Club. When we got divorced, I got all of the Colorado investments and he got all of Las Vegas investments. Before I moved here my ex told me that Mark Willis has been holding out on the other investors and not paying us our share. Let me explain, he was giving us the money from the club, but not our share of the client profits. He was keeping those profits for himself. You see Mark and I never met until I started working for him, and taking care of the books and also the hiring the employees. That is when I decided to blackmail the clients into paying me, not Mark. Victor found out what I was doing, so I took him on as a partner to keep an eye on him and so he would keep his mouth shut. Then I found out that we were not the only ones blackmailing the clients. We found out that the clients were paying Mark to have sex with the dancers at the club and that Sharron Jenkins and her boyfriend were also blackmailing the club. I did what I had to do," Sophia said.

"So you killed her?" Candy asked.

"She was stealing my money…so I had Victor play lovers with her and when I knew the time was right…I had him kidnap her and bring her to my house in Central City and we put her in the basement…When Crystal called in the missing person report that is when I had to do something…so I went down in the basement late at night and I stabbed her in the neck, and then in the chest…ha, ha, ha I thought the police would think that she was a hooker and that her trick killed her. Before I went to the airport, we picked up the body. It was around two in the morning when Victor and I dumped her body in the park. I thought that would be the end of it, but then I found out from Crystal that a man was looking for Sharron. So I had to see what he wanted. I found out he was working with Sharron and he was her boyfriend. Well, he had to go also. So I arranged for Victor to do that job, that way he would get his hands dirty and not squeal on me. When Victor told me that the oxygen tank was in Seth's rental car I left the envelope for him at the front desk…"

"What was inside the envelope?" Candy asked with a curious look on her face.

"It was a letter asking for him to meet me at his rental car and I signed Sharron's name to the letter," Sophia answered.

"When I found out that he was dead, that is when your Detectives came into the story. So I couldn't stop there, and I kidnapped Megan and tried to do the same thing to her. Next, I would have made Mark pay for not giving me my money. Then I would own everything, the club the houses, the money and business."

"What about Victor, what would you have done with him?"
"I guess I would have killed him."

Inside the Mirror

Megan went into a deep meditation to heal her body
She saw Robert's truck. She saw Crystal get out and get into the back of the truck. In the back of the truck she cut open a bag. Inside was a man that looked like he had eaten too many Italian meals, he had dark brown hair with a bald spot on the top of his head, he was dressed like he just stepped out of an Italian Mob movie. Crystal pushed the man off the tailgate into the pen and watched the hogs and piglets devour their meal.

Mirror

Megan awoke and found herself lying in a hospital bed. Robert was sitting in a chair beside her bed.
"I was wondering when you would wake up," Robert said when she looked at him.
"What happened? My head hurts."
"You hit your head when you were fighting with Sophia."
"How did you find me?"
"Victor told us that he..,"
"Robert I have to tell you something, I think I may be psychic because I have strange dreams."
"Ok."
"I dream about...I dreamt about Seth and then..,"
"Well I am glad to see you're awake, Miss Sapphire," said a nurse coming into the room interrupting what Megan was saying.

Ruth picked up the phone on her desk before it stopped ringing.
"Hello," Ruth said into the phone.

"Hello this is Sergeant Walsh from the Black Hawk police department. Would you happen to be looking for a Mark Willis of Denver, Colorado?" A man's voice asked.

"Yes, we are looking for Mark Willis," Ruth replied wondering why the Black Hawk police was contacting her.

"We just found his body in the mountains. He was shot in the head with a Smith & Wesson model 60 .357 Magnum."

"I see, are you sure it is him?"

"Yes, his half-brother identified him."

"Okay, thank you for letting us know bye," Ruth hung up the phone and then called JP who was at Sophia's house searching it for evidence.

When JP answered the phone she said

"I need you to look for a Smith & Wesson model 60 .357 Magnum."

"Okay, we will look for one," JP said into the phone.

"Check in her car, because I just got a call from Black Hawk. Mark's body was found. He was shot in the head," Ruth said.

"Okay, I will call you back," JP said and then hung up the phone.

When JP called back Ruth answered the phone.

"Ruth we found one, and it has fingerprints on the handle. I bet they will be a match for Sophia Abbott's," JP said into the phone.

Crystal was sitting in her living room reading the files that she found in the briefcase waiting for her at the post office, when the phone rang on the table next to her. Crystal answered the phone.

"Hello," Crystal said into the phone.

"Miss Stone, it is done," a man's voice said.

"Are you sure it's done?" said Crystal.

"I took care of it personally, Crystal."

"Thank you Mr. Valentine."

"Not a problem. He was a dick, anyway."

"Megan and Robert, I want to thank you for helping us on this case," Ruth said holding up a glass of wine.

"Yes we couldn't have not found Sharron Jenkins killer if it wasn't for you, Megan," Candy said.

"Well, I just wish that it didn't hurt my head so much to get Sophia," Megan said as she put her hand up to her head wrapped with white gauze. She was lying on the sofa, leaning up against Robert's chest.

"Yes and thanks to JP...by the way he is late, where is he?" Robert asked looking at the crowd that was sitting in Megan's living area.

"He should be here, I told him to meet us here," Ruth said taking a sip of her wine.

"Well, anyway you were saying?" Megan said.

"As I was saying, thanks to JP we got a confession out of Victor. We must not forget you, Candy, for getting a confession out of Sophia," Robert said.

"We found out that Sophia killed Mark before we could arrest him for prostitution though..." Candy said but was interrupted at the sound of someone coming into the loft. JP walked into the living area escorting Crystal Stone.

"I am sorry we are late, but we had to stop at the lawyers and then the club," JP said taking Crystal's coat off and putting it on Megan's bed in the bedroom area.

"So, I take it that the lawyer decided to read Mark Willis' will," Ruth said.

"Yes, the will said that I should run the club if anything happened to Victor, Sophia, or Rocco Valentine," Crystal said.

"Mr. Valentine told the lawyer that he didn't want any part of the club or any of his brother's belongings so Crystal gets everything," JP said and then smiled before giving Crystal a kiss and hug.

"So, what are you going to do with the club, Crystal?" Megan asked.

"I am going to make it a concert hall and lounge, with a disco in the back," Crystal said with a smile.

"Well, here is to Mark Willis, no matter if he was a slime ball," JP said after giving Crystal a glass of wine. Crystal clinked her glass with the others as they toasted to Mark.

"And here's to Crystal for getting all of Mark's assets, and also to the end of the case," Megan said.

"Yes, thank you, Mark, thank you for leaving me everything," Crystal said and then laughed as she took a sip of her wine. Though she laughed on the outside, she felt a little more of her die that day.

www.ingramcontent.com/pod-product-compliance
Lightning Source LLC
Chambersburg PA
CBHW060111260626
47160CB00005B/1862